the Darkest Curse

A RAPUNZEL RETELLING

Book 1 in the Nethervale series

RACHEL ROWLANDS

Cover design by Asterielly Designs
Book layout and interior design by Lisa Gilliam
Proofreading by Philip Ridgers

For more information, visit: www.racheljrowlands.com

ISBN: 978-1-7391355-0-8 (paperback)
ISBN: 978-1-7391355-1-5 (ebook)

*To the family and friends who encouraged me
to believe there was more than one path to my
dreams – thank you.*

Table of Contents

Chapter One

Annice spent most of the morning cleaning up any trace of her cursed hair from the tower. If any strands were left when her mother, Gothel, came to visit, the hairs could very well kill her.

By the time Annice was done dusting, mopping, scrubbing and inspecting every inch of the tower for stray black hairs, she was exhausted. Her hair was already wrapped tightly in a silk wrap made especially by Gothel to help keep it from coming into contact with human skin. Flopping onto the loveseat, Annice sighed, lifting her bare feet onto the fabric.

The top of her tower contained a large circular sitting area and library, where she spent most of her time, and a tiny kitchen. The bedroom and small ladies' room were on the floors below.

Annice glanced at the clock on the bookshelf nearby, then sighed and examined the rows upon rows of mahogany bookshelves running along the opposite wall, stacked with leather-bound tomes, most in dusty shades of pink and cream. Gothel would be here soon; she came every day at noon, right on schedule. She needed to ask her to bring her some more novels. She'd read everything she owned, some of them multiple times. She was beginning to wonder if she'd read all the fiction books in the kingdom and was running out. Maybe she'd write her own next. Gothel had given her a beautiful writing desk last year, positioned by the huge window spanning most of the width of the tower, with a view over the lush green forests, rolling hills and rounded trees of the Kingdom of Lumen.

She lifted her lyre from the corner of the loveseat, placed the wooden surface against her and began to pluck the strings, playing a tune she'd recently put together. The melodic sounds resonated around the room, filling the silence, but she still felt an ache of loneliness in her chest, as she did most days.

A slamming sound echoed up from below, and Annice paused her playing to listen as footsteps drew closer.

"Annice!" called Gothel's voice, echoing up the winding stairway. She was the only one who had a key to the tower's main door below.

Annice didn't reply until Gothel was framed in the doorway. "Hi, Mother," she said.

A silver key gleamed on a cord around Gothel's neck. Gothel was tall, pale and black haired; she liked to joke that at least they looked like true mother and daughter now, since Annice's hair had been cursed and turned black. But where Annice's hair was sleek and straight and fell to the floor smoothly, Gothel's was curly and wild, like tangled branches clawing across a forest.

"How are you today, darling?" Gothel said. As Annice stood to greet her, Gothel swept in and planted a kiss on her cheek.

"I wish you wouldn't do that," said Annice. "You never know if there's a stray hair on my cheek." Her hair could kill any living thing it touched. It was why she'd spent almost her whole life in this tower, locked away from the world. The curse on her hair only affected other living things – people, plants and animals – not herself. And there was no point trying to cut it off, either. It just grew back quickly and fiercely.

"I'm sure you were very thorough. You always are." Gothel lifted a basket covered in a striped cloth. "I brought a few things."

"Any books?" Annice asked eagerly.

"Oh, not this time. You didn't ask for any."

Annice sighed. "Can you get me some more books? Ones I haven't read?"

"I can never keep up with what you have and haven't read, my dear."

This was true. She'd brought duplicates many times. It was one of the many things that frustrated Annice about being trapped in this tower: not being able to pick out her own clothes, her own books, her own *anything*.

"Don't look at me like that, pet," said Gothel. She patted Annice on the arm. "You know I do my best."

"I know. Sorry. Have you found any—?"

"Any more apothecaries? My dear. Must you ask me this question every time? There are only three in the kingdom, and they know nothing of the rampion wildflower's curse, or how to treat it. You know I don't have the money to go overseas to consult with anyone else. I'm doing my best to save coin."

"Someone must know something," said Annice.

"I'm sure we could work with someone eventually, when we've enough money," said Gothel gently. She came closer, smiling softly at Annice, who felt awful for interrogating her – but she couldn't help it. She lived for the hope that one day, Gothel would step in and say she'd had a breakthrough, or some apothecary had come up with a cure for her affliction. "Look in the basket!" Gothel went on, her piercing blue eyes sparkling. "We can have a lovely lunchtime treat on the balcony."

"Alright." Annice smiled back at her mother and settled on the loveseat, pulling the striped cloth from the basket.

She gasped in delight when she looked inside. A jar of lush, red strawberry jam; freshly baked bread rolls; bright yellow butter in a glass dish; a mountain of fat strawberries sitting in a bowl.

"Strawberries!" Annice cried – they were one of her favourite fruits.

"They're in season. I thought you'd be happy about it. Do you want to set up on the balcony, and I'll fetch some apple juice from downstairs?"

Annice nodded, taking the basket to the wooden door leading to the balcony. Outside, warm sunlight was spilling onto the side of the tower, washing the stone beneath her feet in luminous yellow. There were two chairs and a low wicker table out here; she ate lunch frequently on the balcony with Gothel in the summer, when the weather grew warmer. Annice spread the fruit, jam and butter out on the table, taking a seat and smoothing her dress before Gothel returned with a pitcher of apple juice and two goblets.

"Here you are," said Gothel, pouring Annice a glass of juice and handing it to her.

"Thank you."

The sun was warm on her arms and face, and she could hear birds singing in the distant trees. Looking out across the balcony, she saw the sky was perfectly blue – not a cloud in the sky. For a fleeting moment, she imagined she was sitting out here with a man she'd fallen in love with, not Gothel. They would spend the day wrapped up in each other's arms until the sun went down and stars emerged one by one. Afterwards, they'd leave the tower, ride off on horseback to some distant land, where they'd have adventures together and see the world of Nethervale. She sighed, watching a white bird swing in an arc across the stretch of blue sky.

"Don't sound so glum," said Gothel, taking a seat opposite and pouring herself a glass of juice. "I thought the strawberries would cheer you up."

"They did, but…"

She didn't quite know how to explain. What she was feeling couldn't be solved with strawberries and bread rolls. She was tired of the same routine: waking and reading her novels, cleaning the tower from top to bottom for Gothel's arrival, spending much of the afternoon with her, playing her lyre and composing in the evenings. There was no room for spontaneous journeys, or for anything more adventurous. She longed to know what was beyond the horizon outside of these walls, what life was like away from her tower.

"Things will get better," Gothel said. "One day, we'll find our answer. Until then, you have to be patient and trust me."

But what if we don't find the answer? Annice didn't ask the question out loud; she needn't bother. She knew they both held it in the back of their minds, a horrible possibility neither of them wanted to voice. That she'd be trapped in this tower forever and would never live an ordinary life. It was nearly her twenty-first birthday, and she hadn't lived any of the milestones she read about in her books: travelling, best friends, first kisses, courting, engagements, serious relationships, sex. She'd read newspapers brought by bluebird messenger, and she wasn't a prude: she'd seen the love advice pages, and tried to apply the recommendations to her own situation, and she'd read enough love stories. She knew how to please herself – and she did. Fulfilling herself was her only option. She just wondered if she'd ever have anyone else. And if she'd ever be able to see the rest of Nethervale.

"I know you're desperate to see the outside world," said Gothel, interrupting her thoughts. "I'm aware books aren't enough. I only hope I can give you the real world someday, and that we'll find a cure for the rampion's dark magic."

Annice took a sip of cold apple juice from her glass to avoid answering. Hope was all they had, but sometimes it was difficult to keep hold of.

They avoided the subject of the rampion wildflower and its magic for the rest of the afternoon. Instead, they talked about what they usually did: Gothel told her all the gossip she'd heard, and detailed her trips to the centre of the kingdom; Annice in turn told her about the books she'd read recently, her favourite characters and plot twists.

When Gothel left, Annice walked down the winding stairs with her to the bottom of the tower, now shaded in slight darkness. Gothel took the key from around her neck, unlocking the door and pushing it open. The sunlight outside was fading as the sun sank lower behind the trees, but Annice could feel the cool breeze on her arms and cheeks. She always walked

Gothel to the bottom so she could catch a glimpse of the outside world: the grass rippling in the wind like the folds of a skirt, the branches of the forest swaying like arms, crickets chirping somewhere in the undergrowth.

"Until tomorrow, then," said Gothel, smiling over her shoulder at Annice.

"Yes, see you tomorrow."

"I'll see what I can do about the books in the morning."

Annice waved her off. Gothel pulled the door closed. It banged shut, cutting off the view of the landscape, eliminating the breeze and silencing the insects. The sound of the door slamming echoed up the stairway, and she was thrown into darkness.

Heaving a sigh, Annice hauled herself back upstairs in the gloom, careful not to trip over her dress as she went. The silence of upstairs was deafening as she stepped back into her library and sitting room. Through the wide window built into the stone side of the tower, she could see the orange sunset blazing behind a line of trees, the scudding clouds pink as they washed across the sky, promising another beautiful day tomorrow.

She padded across the wooden floor, back to the loveseat, and unwrapped her hair. The wraps could hurt after a while, when she wore them too long, since she had so much hair to pile atop her head. Once her hair was cascading down her back again, and she'd folded the silk wrap, she reached for her lyre. It was always within arm's reach. She wanted to practise the song she'd been composing. She strummed and plucked at the strings until the sounds reverberated around the room, and as she played, she stood up, moving around the room. She bobbed in time to the music, humming.

The quiet of the forest outside the tower was disrupted by loud pounding sounds, growing louder over her music. Frowning, Annice halted and let her fingers drop. What *was* that sound? Once, she'd seen the queen's guard coming back from an outing through the forest: dozens of horses and soldiers speeding through the trees. It sounded like that. But the queen's guard rarely came this way; there were much faster paths to the centre of the kingdom.

Annice hurried to her balcony to see what was going on. The hoofbeat sounds had slowed considerably. Maybe whoever it was were leaving the clearing? Gothel had always told her to be careful of outsiders – anyone who expressed an interest in Annice would be putting themselves at risk if they tried to get close to her. But she so rarely saw other people outside of her mother, she couldn't help but lean over the edge of her balcony to see if anyone was still there.

"Hello there!" called a man's voice. "Was that you playing the beautiful music?"

Chapter Two

nnice froze. Down below the tower, amongst the wildflowers and grasses, were two beautiful horses: one as white as the moon with a few sandy patches dappled across its neck and rump, the other several shades darker with a grey mane. They were fully saddled up, but the two men they'd been carrying were standing a few paces in front of them, looking up at her.

One of them had long brown hair skirting his chin, and a beard that gave him a slightly ruffian look. There was a cheeky smirk on his face. The second man looked slightly younger, with curly reddish-brown hair; he was wearing a flamboyant tunic, splashed with striped colours and glitter.

"I'm Cyrus!" called the long-haired man, waving up at her. Unlike his companion, he didn't appear to have a taste for extravagant colours: his tunic was linen and belted at the waist. There was a sword in a sheath at his hip, and something else she couldn't quite make out from up here. "This is Bellamy!" Cyrus added, gesturing at his redheaded friend. "We heard your music and couldn't help stopping."

Finally managing to move, Annice drew back into the shade of the balcony, holding her breath and pressing her back against the stone wall. They were talking too much; she shouldn't have let them see her in the first place. What would Gothel say? She could imagine the warnings spilling from her. *Be careful not to engage with anyone. You know you'd put any friends you made in danger. It's for their own good, darling, that you keep to yourself.*

But the long-haired man… She hadn't been able to see his features completely from her position in the tower, but he looked handsome. And there was a friendliness to his voice that made her heart lift – he'd introduced himself like he wanted to know her. The lilt to his tone had been like sunshine. She wanted to hear more of it.

Annice shook her head roughly. She couldn't. It was too dangerous.

The man was yelling again. "I'm a bard, my friend here's a musician – plays the flute! We're sorry if we scared you, we wanted to meet whoever was playing that beautiful music."

Beautiful? Her music? A flush crept along her cheekbones. It was the song she'd been working on for weeks. She had no one to share her songs with outside of Gothel, and she was sure Gothel only complimented them because it was her duty as a mother.

Annice longed to rush back to the edge of the balcony, to lean over and talk to them both. He'd said he was a bard; did he play music too, or just write? Did he help his friend compose music? Where did they perform? Were they travelling musicians? Her heart sank. If they were, they were probably passing through.

It's for the best, she told herself. *Let them go.*

She clamped her lips together to keep herself from calling back to them.

"We're sorry to have scared you!" called that familiar, sunshine-lilting voice.

A quietness settled over the clearing, and soon hoofbeats sounded again, fading into the distance.

———

She barely slept the next few nights, replaying the memory of leaning over and hearing Cyrus talk to her over and over again. She imagined how the conversation would have gone if she'd answered, or if her hair hadn't been cursed. She might have gone down to them, had a picnic with them on the grass. They could have played together. She might have gone with them to a tavern to sing and dance and make music, drinking wine and laughing into the night. They would have become friends, and then she and Cyrus, perhaps something more.

When the sunlight finally crept into her bedroom on one of the lower floors of the tower, a few mornings later, she'd slept perhaps a couple of hours, at most. She was so distracted recently, unable to quiet her mind at night as she usually did, and unable to focus on reading for more than twenty minutes at a time. It was still close to daybreak, and she normally didn't rise so early, but she got up anyway, wrapped her hair and began her morning ritual of cleaning and scouting the tower for loose hairs in preparation for Gothel's arrival.

Unlike most days when Gothel visited, she was done with her ritual early because she'd risen with the sun. She sat on the balcony in a patch of shade with one of her novels, her feet up on a velvet cushion and a glass of squeezed orange juice by her side. The sun was bright and beaming today, so she'd put on a wide-brimmed hat to shield her eyes.

She was just starting to feel deeply engrossed in the story and the characters, and was smiling at their antics, when she heard hoofbeats down in the clearing below. Annice scrambled upright from where she'd slumped in her chair, and almost dropped her book.

"Cyrus again?" she mumbled. She wasn't sure if her palms were sweating from the sun or from nerves. What was she going to do if he tried to talk to her again?

She decided to risk a peek over the edge of the balcony.

She saw only one horse on the bright grass. As she watched, half-crouching, the man swung his legs out of the saddle and dismounted. His bright orange and yellow tunic blazed in the sun, threaded with gold stars. It wasn't Cyrus; it was his companion Bellamy.

Gothel would be here soon. She hoped Bellamy would go away before she got here. He'd only get in trouble with her mother if he stayed, and she could have a fierce temper when it suited her. She'd screamed at some children who had tried to climb the tower's vines once, when Annice was very young. They'd never returned.

"Are you there, miss?" Bellamy was calling up to her.

"Curses," she hissed. Well, maybe it was no good cowering on her balcony as if she were a frightened child. It wouldn't put a stop to these visits. She'd have to be more like Gothel – stern, hard. This was *her* tower, after all. Her home. She straightened up, squared her shoulders and leaned forwards so he could see her, looking down.

"What do you want?" she called back. "Why do you keep disturbing me?"

"Oh!" He grasped a hand to his chest and laughed in surprise; he hadn't been expecting her to answer. Her lips quirked at the thought that she hadn't been entirely predictable. "I'm sorry!" he said. "I came to ask if you'd mind meeting with my friend Cyrus?"

Annice knitted her eyebrows together. "Meet him?"

"Yes! He hasn't stopped talking about you these past days… He's enchanted by you, by your music."

Enchanted by me? Annice blinked, but she couldn't help the rushing feeling in her belly, as though she'd missed a step walking down the tower staircase.

"Why… why didn't he come here himself?" she asked, then wished she hadn't spoken. She shouldn't be encouraging more visits – Gothel wouldn't like it and it wasn't safe. But her heart was pounding with excitement. Cyrus found her enchanting. And she was talking to someone new, someone other than Gothel.

"He didn't want to bother you," Bellamy replied. "He thought it would be… rude of him, invasive."

Be hard, Annice told herself. *Be like Gothel.*

"Well, it would," she said. "This is my tower."

"That's why he sent me to ask you instead. And if you aren't interested, simply say so, and I promise we won't come back. But, if I may say so, miss…" He gave her a wide grin, his bright white teeth slightly pointed, making him look even more cheeky and young than he did already. "Your music is lovely. We've been hoping to add another member to our troupe – but Cyrus is very particular."

Annice hesitated. She could feel the hardness she was trying to maintain crumbling in the wake of all these promises: she could have conversations about music and art, things Gothel didn't tend to appreciate – she preferred herbs and botany. She could form friendships with people with similar interests. She'd never had a friend.

But this wouldn't be good for them. She couldn't have them coming here. At the same time, she didn't want to let them go. She knew she'd regret it forever if she did. Letters couldn't hurt, could they? There was no physical contact that way, so there was no risk of her hair doing any harm. It also avoided the problem of them turning up at the tower when Gothel was due to arrive.

"I won't meet with him," she told Bellamy, "but… tell him he can write to me here, at the tower, by bluebird messenger."

Bellamy surprised her this time. He jumped up and down like a boy and clapped his hands together, giving a laugh that rang out to her and made a smile form on her own face.

"He'll be so pleased!" Bellamy cried. "I'll tell him right away, miss… What's your name?"

Her smile grew wider. "It's Annice."

—◦◦◦—

That night, she was so eager for a letter to arrive that she waited in her sitting room and library long past the point of being tired. She hadn't drawn the curtains over the window, and the sickle moon hung in the sky, yellow as a buttercup, surrounded by a dotting of silver stars. Annice had a book open in her lap, but she could barely read two sentences, as she kept glancing up to see if a bluebird had flitted across the sky, or landed on her balcony.

She soon fell asleep with her head in the book. When she woke, it was already morning, but there was no letter and no bluebird waiting for her.

Annice went about her usual ritual of preparing for Gothel's visit, but she was distracted; she kept pausing to check the balcony for signs of the bluebird. She'd only just finished cleaning up and wrapping her hair when Gothel arrived, and of course her mother could tell she was distracted.

"You seem even more daydreamy than usual today, my dear," Gothel said carefully. She'd brought Annice some more books – the basket on the table was full of them, each spine a dusty shade of lilac, pink and coral with looping gold or silver titles.

"Thinking about a project," said Annice, tearing her gaze away from the wide tower window and the fluffy white clouds.

"Your song?"

"No." Annice had to resist bursting into a grin; she kept her voice level. "Actually… a writing project, this time. A romance story I want to write."

"Oh. I see," said Gothel. "I'm glad you have things to occupy your time. I have some things to do at the flower shop, orders have been coming in quickly. But I know you need me here, and I don't want to spend less time with you."

"I'm nearly twenty-one. I'm not a child. You're

welcome to a life of your own," Annice insisted. But now Gothel was saying all this, she was feeling a dull disappointment. She wanted to be able to have a life, too. To meet someone at a café, to eat cakes and go for a stroll along the river afterwards, buy flowers.

"You don't need to worry about me, Mother," said Annice, pushing down her feelings. "I know you work hard to look after us both."

Gothel smiled. "Your father would be so proud of the woman you've become, Annice. He…"

She trailed off. Gothel always hesitated when she spoke about Annice's father, even though the subject didn't bother Annice. But Annice suspected it was too painful for her to discuss. As a toddler, Annice had eaten a sprig of wild rampion one day – sometimes called the rapunzel plant – spawning the curse on her hair. Her father was desperate to work with Gothel to find a cure, but he died shortly after of a sickness, and never got the chance.

"You enjoy this writing project of yours," said Gothel, changing the subject. "I hope you'll let me read it sometime."

"Of course."

Gothel smiled, looking more relaxed.

When she'd gone, Annice saw her off as usual at the door to the tower. Once it had clunked shut, she raced up to the top again to check the balcony for any bluebird messenger, but a quick glimpse showed nothing. Sighing, she turned to go back inside, dragging her feet in disappointment.

A chirp behind her made her heart leap into her throat. She wheeled round, nearly tripping over her skirts as she went.

There, perched on the back of her chair out on the balcony, was a tiny cerulean bird, its chest puffed out proudly, a letter clamped into its beak. They were such small things, these letter carriers, but they were remarkably strong thanks to the magic they possessed; they could even carry bundles of newspapers and thick books. The bird turned its shiny crystalline eyes on her and chirped again, flittering to the table and dropping the letter.

Annice raced outside to snatch up the cream-coloured envelope. The little bird sat watching her. They always waited to see if you wanted to respond to anything before flying away.

Beaming, she hurried inside to sit at her writing desk, slicing open the envelope with her letter opener. She'd only ever used it to open letters from Gothel, who rarely wrote to her – only when she went further afield on a shopping trip and would be gone a few days – and her physician, who consulted with her by letter.

With shaking fingers, she tugged out the folded, thick paper inside. Smoothing out the paper, she saw Cyrus's handwriting was neat and looping, slightly slanted across the page. He drew his I's in curling loops that were almost artistic.

Dear Annice,

Bellamy tells me it's alright that I write to you. Thank you for that. We loved your music, and by the light, how I wanted to talk with the person making those sounds! Do you have a tutor? How long have you been playing? Do you live alone in the tower, or is there a dragon guarding the stairway? I'm joking. I hope I haven't asked too many questions.

Speaking of dragons, do you know one of the tales I regularly perform as a poem is about a dragon-slaying I witnessed for myself? I even made up a dance to go with the story. Unfortunately, I wasn't the one who killed the dragon, and it wasn't that exiting. They're friendly creatures these days, domesticated. It was just very unwell and needed to be at peace. We embellished the story for entertainment. It was Bellamy's idea. So I can't impress you with that story!

Faithfully,
Cyrus Lockwood

She read the letter so quickly the first time she felt she had to go back and read it again, more slowly, to absorb every penned word. When she'd read it a third time, she laughed. She wondered what his tale was like, how it sounded when put alongside music and dance.

It took her five drafts to get her response right; she feared the bluebird might be gone by the time she was done. She kept scribbling things out that didn't sound right, or things that sounded too awkward. Finally, she settled on:

Dear Cyrus,

Thank you for your letter. I'm so glad someone likes my music. I don't have a tutor. I'm self-taught and have been playing since I was five. Writing a poem sounds fun. I'm not much of a poet, but I'd like to hear yours in future. I don't leave my tower much, though, so you're unlikely to find me in a tavern or in Firefly Square.

You and Bellamy sound fascinating. I'm keen to hear more about what you do. Do you travel all over Nethervale? Are you from the Kingdom of Lumen or overseas? Do you play an instrument yourself? And do you really know how to use the sword you wear on your hip?

Respectfully,
Annice Au'vair

The tiny bird was still there – it had moved into the tower without her noticing, perched on a bookshelf, watching her write. She folded her letter neatly and placed it in a fresh envelope from her writing set, before sliding it into the bird's beak. Its task complete, the bird spread its wings and took flight, soaring through the window.

"Thank you!" Annice called after it, waving.

She heard a trilling chirp in response.

Annice hurried onto the balcony to watch it flit away, wondering how long it'd be before another letter from Cyrus arrived.

—◦◦◦—

The day of Annice's twenty-first birthday dawned bright and sunny, like most other summer days in the Kingdom of Lumen. She'd expected to wake feeling heavy, having such an important birthday with no cure in sight, still locked in her tower. But instead, she felt light and breezy as the day outside. She'd exchanged a few more letters with Cyrus since their first correspondence. He'd told her they had a few taverns to play at – they were travellers after all – and in turn she'd mentioned her birthday. When he'd asked if she had any plans, she simply said she wasn't sure.

As always, Gothel turned up at close to noon after Annice had completed her chores. She wore a regal purple dress that fell to her knees, with matching heels, and she'd adorned her hair with a smooth silk band to push it back from her face.

"Happy birthday, my dear." She kissed Annice's hand and squeezed it hard. Normally, she only brought her shopping basket, but today she'd brought the basket and a number of brown paper bags. "Presents!" she trilled, gesturing at them. "And I brought a birthday cake, some wine… Shall we enjoy them on the balcony?"

Annice couldn't avoid the slight sinking feeling in her gut. Although she enjoyed sitting on her balcony in the sunshine, it was what she did regularly in the summertime. She wanted to do something different today. Something special for her birthday, even though she knew it wasn't possible in the circumstances. She tried to hide her disappointment by taking the presents out onto the balcony, while Gothel went to fetch plates and glasses from her tiny kitchen.

Soon they had a birthday feast set up: Gothel had brought finger sandwiches stuffed with spiced meat, thick cheese pastries, fat purple grapes, ginger biscuits and, best of all, a luxurious birthday cake in three tiers. She'd placed it at the centre of the table they sat around on the balcony, all white icing and pink and purple flowers, with the number twenty-one drawn on the top in loopy gold. It looked delicious, although far too large for two people, and Annice felt a pang, wishing she had others to share it with. Cyrus and his friend Bellamy might like it.

"Aren't you hungry, my dear?" Gothel asked. She was

already tucking into a cheese pastry. "Well, in any case, open some presents! I want to see your face."

The thought of presents perked Annice up – small joys she could still appreciate, even trapped in a tower as she was. She tore through the brown paper bags.

"How did you afford all this?" she asked as she went. "You shouldn't have."

Gothel waved a hand. "I can always spare something for your birthday, my dear. Don't worry. I'm frugal. I'll be able to get overseas eventually to help search for your cure. You know how expensive foreign travel is."

Annice nodded. The first bag contained a beautiful powder-pink gown, with roses stitched across the skirt and neckline in paler shades of pink-white.

"It's beautiful," Annice breathed, holding it up.

"Keep going!" said Gothel, finishing her pastry and dusting crumbs from her fingers.

Inside the other paper bags were a couple more books, a beautiful new silk bathrobe, some scented candles that smelt like strawberry and cakes, and a sparkling silver hairclip shaped like a crescent moon.

"Thank you," Annice breathed, running her hands over the clip. "These are all wonderful gifts."

"I'm glad you like them. I know you didn't choose this life, my darling. The least I can do is make sure you're comfortable, and happy with what you have."

With what I have... Annice couldn't deny that her things were lovely. She was lucky to have a room full of books, a bed to sleep in, food to eat and an instrument to play. But she still felt trapped, imprisoned here, while the world outside went on without her. It was as if she were frozen in time, except she was still aging. One day, she'd run out of time, and no one would remember she'd been here, a girl playing her lyre at the top of the tower. The thought made her suddenly sombre, and she had to force the smile she offered Gothel.

"I am grateful," she said carefully – because she was. Her mother Gothel had done nothing but provide for her. She adjusted the hair wrap by her ear and went on, "But it feels like we'll never find a cure with me stuck in this tower, even with you helping."

Gothel's smile faded. "What would you suggest?" she said sharply. "You can't leave the tower yourself. You know that."

Annice drew in a breath, considering her words carefully. Gothel was like a thorn at the centre of a bush – not dangerous if you kept away from it and admired the bush from afar, but sharp if pricked. "If I wrapped my hair carefully, like I do when you visit—"

"Out of the question," Gothel cut across her. She already appeared irritated, even though Annice had been cautious with her wording.

"But—"

"Annice, think of it this way. If you went outside with your hair wrapped, what then? You go somewhere. What if someone bumps into you and the hair wrap falls off? What if it's windy and it comes undone? If your hair brushes grass, it will blacken and die. Trees would wither. And a person? If too much of your hair touched them, the curse would spread through their veins, black and toxic – and kill them."

Annice flinched.

"I know we've made little progress and you're frustrated," Gothel continued, "but I've asked you to trust me. It's my responsibility to keep you safe."

"I know it is. I just—"

"It's too risky to have you wandering around."

Annice felt a prickle of annoyance; she was trying to speak and Gothel kept talking over her. She wasn't a child anymore and she felt she had a right to be heard, to have some say in her own life.

"Just listen!" Annice burst out. Gothel looked shocked, so she rushed on while she had the chance: "We've made no progress, all this time. All these *years*. I know you're saving up to go overseas. But aren't we being *too* safe? Maybe taking risks would work, it's the only thing we haven't tried!"

"No." Gothel's voice was firm, and hard as a boulder. "I won't take risks, not with you. You're too important to me."

Annice sat back in her seat, staring at the birthday cake and its smooth white icing. She didn't understand. She'd always been concerned about keeping other people safe from her hair, but today she was having other thoughts. If she were cautious, wrapped her hair carefully, and avoided crowded places such as the centre of the kingdom and the square, *could* she go outside? Gothel had never allowed her to try, so how would they know if it was safe or not? They had no evidence either way.

"Sorry, Annice, but that's final." Gothel's eyes were hard, and devoid of any emotion – even sympathy.

Annice frowned back at her, then looked down at the cake, and the looping letters spelling out her age. Wasn't she old enough to make her own choices now? She bit her lip, conflicted. Gothel had only ever wanted to protect her, and others. Maybe she was being foolish, letting her birthday and Cyrus's letters impair her thinking.

But even after Gothel left, and they'd eaten several slices of birthday cake, she couldn't stop thinking about the outside world, and what it might be like to step further into it.

—⟳⟳⟳—

Annice kept up her letters to Cyrus, and soon they were in a back-and-forth correspondence. She learned he didn't play an instrument, just wrote poetry and appreciated music, which was why he needed Bellamy to assist him when they performed. They were old friends, he told her, and had known each other since childhood, growing up in the same village. She imagined how lovely it must be to have such a long-lasting friendship, but it made her sad, too, because it was something she didn't think she'd ever experience. Cyrus also told her he could indeed use the sword at his hip, although he preferred not to. There were dangerous creatures in some parts of the Kingdom of Lumen, so travellers needed to be able to protect themselves.

In turn, she told him about her book collection, how she loved anticipating a new story. She talked him through her process of developing an idea for a piece of music, and how she'd sometimes wake in the night feeling inspired, unable to sleep, and would play her lyre on the balcony until the urge was satisfied.

The more she talked to Cyrus by letter, the more she wanted to see him, to talk properly – in person.

It couldn't do any harm if he stayed at the bottom of the tower and she at the top, could it? Gothel was only ever concerned about her hair killing the grass, or hurting a living being. If she stayed up here out of reach, Cyrus would be safe from her hair, and none of them would have to worry.

She still hadn't told Cyrus about her hair, though. The guilt that she'd been keeping a secret gnawed at her, and she knew she'd have to do it eventually. He would wonder why she never left her tower.

Dear Cyrus, she wrote back another day. *I'd like to see you and talk properly, but I have a few conditions. My tower will remain locked. You can talk to me from the clearing below. I know this might be inconvenient to you, but that's what I'd ask.*

He wrote back, and she couldn't help jumping around her sitting room when she read the response: *I would be delighted. And of course. I'll do whatever makes you comfortable.*

Her heart felt like it might burst. All these years of reading books and dreaming she could have friends and now she had a chance.

Annice carefully arranged the day Cyrus would visit so it coincided with a day Gothel would be working at the flower shop. Gothel wouldn't be visiting Annice that day, and Annice had made sure she made it clear that it was absolutely fine with her.

When the day dawned, it was freeing that she didn't have to perform her usual ritual of removing any loose hairs from her sitting room and library and making sure her hair was neatly wrapped. She felt positively silly – she even jumped up and down on her loveseat, purposefully shaking out her hair so it bounced around her body and waved like the sea. Today she didn't need to hide it away, or to be cautious.

She waited on her balcony, barefoot, at the appointed time. She was wearing the new dress Gothel had bought her for her birthday, and she kept impulsively smoothing the pink material and stitched roses. She'd never had an occasion to do her hair, only wrap it, so she'd weaved it into a long braid and pinned on the moon-shaped clip.

Annice kept her eyes fixed on the treeline, listening intently for the sound of hooves or the tell-tale sign of a silhouette moving through the trees. When she heard the horse approaching, she stiffened, mouth suddenly dry, and took a sip of grape juice from the glass on the table behind her.

Cyrus was here.

Chapter Three

Cyrus cantered into the clearing on his horse. He was wearing a tunic again, this time in moss green, and his hair shone and gleamed in the sun as he approached the tower. The horse's hooves beat across the grass, and he reined it to a stop close to the tower and grinned up at her balcony, waving.

"Morning!" he called up.

"H-Hello!" she tried, and had to repeat it louder when she realised she'd barely breathed the word, and he wouldn't be able to hear from down there.

Cyrus swung himself off his horse and tied the reins to a nearby tree before coming to stand where she could see him.

He stood tall, looking confident, and her stomach flip-flopped. His sword was at his hip as usual and his boots were shiny as if freshly polished. She hadn't noticed the soft shape of his jaw before, and wondered what it'd be like to run her fingers along it.

"Thanks for agreeing to meet with me," he called up to her. He sounded soft, gentle, and there was a warmth to his tone.

"I'm happy to talk to you properly," she answered, trying to control her shaking voice.

"You have a lovely voice. Can you sing?"

"Somewhat. I'm not the best singer, even though I enjoy it. I'm better at the lyre and writing." It was far easier to talk to him than she'd imagined. She'd thought she'd be stumbling over her words, struggling to have a conversation with anyone who wasn't her mother. But his gentle voice encouraged her, made her feel safe.

"Why not sing me a song?" he said light-heartedly.

"Oh, no!" She waved her hands in dismissal, feeling her cheeks heat. "I couldn't!"

"No pressure!" He laughed, and the sound trilled up to her, making her smile. "You have to build up to performing."

His laugh had made her feel even more confident. Her voice no longer trembled when she answered. "I can't imagine ever performing. What's it like?"

"Nerve-wracking at first. But I've been doing it a few years now with Bellamy, and now it's just fun. We love it."

"It sounds like you have an amazing life. Travelling and playing music sounds like a dream."

"We're lucky. Things weren't always so easy." He hesitated. She wondered what he meant, but didn't feel it was appropriate to ask. "What about you?" he asked her. "I don't know much about your life, except that you live here."

"There isn't much to tell."

She'd hoped the conversation wouldn't go this way, not yet. Was it wrong to have invited him here? Would he run when he learned of her curse? They wouldn't be as interested in her when they found out about the rampion, would they? If they knew she couldn't ever meet them properly, that she couldn't join their troupe or play with them, would they keep coming back to see her? She thought it unlikely. Doubt crawled across her skin.

Maybe it was best to be honest. Gothel had a saying: *Rip the bandage off quickly*. If she told him now, he'd go away, and he'd be safe. It would hurt, but she'd rather hurt herself emotionally than risk killing someone with her curse.

She'd been kidding herself, trying to befriend Cyrus and Bellamy and hoping for something more. She'd never be able to have what other people had.

She inhaled a large breath. *Tell him*. "I don't have much of a life, outside of music and books. I'm shut up in this tower all the time. My mother has to bring me food."

Cyrus cocked his head to one side. "Why?"

"I'm cursed by the rampion's dark magic." She

gestured at her head, at the moon-shaped clip shining yellow in the sunlight. "It's how my hair became black – the flower only grows in soil infused with dark magic. If my hair touched you, it'd kill you."

There was a silence, filled only with the chittering of birds in the trees and a gull flying over the tower. Cyrus's horse puffed air through its nostrils and stamped its hoof onto the grass.

His answer seemed to take an age to come. To Annice's surprise, she felt lighter. Like she'd been carrying steel on her shoulders and had been released from the burden.

"Is that why you've been so hesitant?" Cyrus asked.

She stared down at him, processing the words. Was that all he had to say? She'd expected him to make an excuse to clamber hastily back onto his horse and disappear into the sun. Or at the very least to express shock. But he was standing with one hand planted casually on his hip, the other hanging at his side, and he was still looking up at her, the wind whispering through his hair.

"Well, of course!" she called down to him. "I don't let myself get close to anyone except my mother, and even that requires *hours* of preparation. Hair wrapping, cleaning…"

"You never leave this tower?"

"No. I need to protect people from me."

"Can't you just… cut it off?" He made a gesture with his hand, towards his own hair.

"We've tried. It doesn't work like that. It's part of the curse. It grows back overnight to its original length."

"You said you wrap your hair to protect your mother. Yet you still never leave? Not even for walks?" Now he was sounding shocked, but not because of the curse, she gathered. "You live in such a beautiful forest and you haven't explored it? Couldn't you wrap your hair just to go for a walk? There's some beautiful waterfalls five minutes from here."

She hadn't known that. She could feel the warm blush creeping onto her cheeks. She'd only ever seen natural wonders in books. What she could see from her tower – birds, deer, trees, the weather – was as far as her experience went.

"I'd love to," she said. "I just can't risk it. If my hair fell out of the wrap… I could kill the grass, the wildlife, the trees…"

He nodded, but crossed his arms, as if thinking. "It must be lonely," he said. "Up there on your own. Your mother doesn't live there, then?"

"No. It's too dangerous." The words caught in her throat. *It must be lonely.* Even Gothel never said those exact words. She was always so positive and encouraging, but sometimes the crushing weight of loneliness on Annice's chest was too much. And Gothel never really acknowledged it. "It is lonely sometimes," she admitted, wondering why in the kingdom she was sharing this with someone she'd only just met.

"I can understand what you mean."

"You can?" She arched her brows, even though he couldn't see the action from down there. She found it hard to imagine that a travelling bard, adventuring with a good friend, would experience loneliness. He must be around people all the time when he was performing.

"Of course. I travel, so I'm often far away from family, from my own mother," he explained. "And sometimes you can be surrounded by people and still feel lonely. I'm not stuck in a tower, but I can understand how you feel."

"I… see." She wondered if there were more to it. He seemed to be holding back, and his head was tilted towards the forest now, away from her. They hardly knew each other, so she wasn't going to ask for more details. But her heart felt warm. He understood her, this stranger who had come into her forest and been drawn by her music. She'd never felt understood before; with Gothel it always felt like a battle to put her point across.

"Would you play for me?" he asked suddenly. "I'd enjoy hearing your music again."

"I… What shall I play?"

"Something of your own."

Her new piece? Her cheeks and neck flamed. She'd never had an audience before outside of Gothel. The flutter in her stomach was part excitement, part nerves. She was close to saying no, because she was anxious, but something held her back. Cyrus had landed on her doorstep unexpectedly, and she was being offered opportunities she might not have had before – to play for someone. Wasn't this what she'd always wanted? While her mind urged her to refuse, to retreat – screaming that it was dangerous to befriend him, and this could be embarrassing too – her heart said something else. Hadn't she been telling Gothel that sometimes a risk might be worth it, because they'd played it safe for far too long?

Maybe she should listen to her own advice. She didn't want to grow old and die in this tower without feeling like she'd lived, in any way she could. And if it meant setting aside her nerves and playing music for a man from her balcony, then she would do it.

"Give me a moment!" she called.

Hurrying back into the tower, she grabbed her lyre. She hadn't finished the piece yet, but she could play him what she had so far. She didn't need anything else, but she stood in the middle of the room for a moment to compose herself, pulling in several deep breaths and pressing a hand to her heart. It was pounding furiously.

"It'll be okay," she breathed to herself. Her palms were sweating so she wiped them on a loose blanket on the loveseat before heading back out onto the balcony.

He was sitting on the grass now, waiting for her, propped up on his elbows. He smiled when she appeared. She couldn't help but beam back. It felt better with him sitting, for some reason. Less formal. Some of her nerves ebbed.

They flowed back full force when she lifted the lyre. Annice took another deep breath, closed her eyes, and began to play.

It helped to keep her eyes shut. She could pretend he wasn't there, that she was alone in her tower, her and the music. Her fingers weaved a pattern across the strings, plucking and tugging, the notes trilling out into the open meadow. In the gaps between notes, she heard his horse snuffling and a flock of birds swoop overhead, chittering as they went. Soon she was absorbed by her melody and gained confidence, picking up pace as the piece neared its middle.

When she'd reached the end — as far as she'd got with this piece — she let go, and it stopped abruptly.

"That's all I have so far," she told him, opening her eyes. She was almost afraid to look down and see his response, but when she did, he was on his feet, and he gave her a round of fierce applause that had his horse's ears pricking back.

She gave a stiff, joking bow and laughed. "Thanks."

He laughed in return, and it sounded so full of delight and appreciation that she clutched the lyre tighter to her chest. "It was wonderful," he said. "You really do have talent."

"Well, I have plenty of time to practise, being stuck here."

They sank into an easy flow of conversation. She told him about the resources she'd used for practising: all the books on music she'd obtained from Gothel, how Gothel had once had a troupe come and play for her in the meadow. She told him about her love of books and she discovered he liked to read adventure stories and travel diaries. He talked about his mother, who lived overseas in the Kingdom of Orinthia – where he and Bellamy came from – and how she owned a bakery and made the best cinnamon rolls. His father, unfortunately, was a drunk, and he'd always hoped his mother would leave, but she clung on. He told her the story of how they'd come to be here in the Kingdom of Lumen, fresh out of school and ready for an adventure. His mother had encouraged him to chase his dreams but most of his peers and teachers thought he'd fail and end up living as a penniless musician, which hadn't been the case in the end.

"It's amazing that you started so young," Annice said wistfully. "And you're still doing it now?"

"Yep. Seven years later. We have quite the reputation and we make a living. We spent the first year or two playing at home, then travelled when we had enough money."

He was twenty-three, two years older than her. He'd already achieved so much. Sadness rose up inside her. She wished she could do all the things she'd wanted to do by twenty-one. She felt like she'd achieved so little and it was a constant ache inside her.

"How long have you been in the Kingdom of Lumen?"

"Six months. We like it here, and the money is good,

so we might stay up to a year or so." He looked back at the sun, where it was moving across the sky. "I should go soon. We have to play at an inn tonight and I need to rehearse with Bellamy." He paused. "Can I come by again?" The rest of his words came out in a rush. "I know you'll be staying inside your tower and your hair is cursed, but… we have so much in common. I like talking to you."

She considered. Could it hurt, to have him return when Gothel was at work? She never had to know. And Annice could make sure Cyrus was safe by having him stay in the meadow, or… Could she wrap her hair up and let him in, like she did with Gothel? Gothel had always discouraged her from having anyone else inside the tower. But if it worked with Gothel, it would surely work with Cyrus too?

She didn't voice this idea to Cyrus yet. She'd think about it.

What she did say was: "You can come back. I'd love to see you again."

His smile was nearly as bright as the sun.

—⟢—

They arranged via letters for Cyrus to return in eight days' time. Gothel had a work outing, visiting some botanical gardens and a winery on the opposite side of the kingdom. She would be gone the entire day.

Annice could barely concentrate on anything in the meantime. Gothel noticed she was distracted but seemed to think it was post-birthday sadness, because she'd reached a milestone age and was still trapped in her tower. Annice didn't correct her. When Gothel wasn't there, she spent most of her time scribbling letters to Cyrus and working on her piece. She weaved in more of how she felt: rising and quickly falling notes for the butterflies she felt when he looked at her, low tones for the aching desire she had to go off adventuring.

When the day came for Cyrus to return, Annice cleaned every inch of the tower, even though Gothel wasn't coming. She wrapped her hair as tightly as she could without giving herself a headache, in a beautiful silvery wrap sheeted with stars. The dress she'd chosen was plain and midnight blue, falling to her ankles, with short puffed sleeves. Tiny pearls adorned her ears. She'd always enjoyed experimenting with make-up, even with nowhere to go, but this time she wore it with purpose, swiping blush onto her cheeks and painting her lips a dusty shade of pink. All the while, her stomach was flocked with butterflies and she could feel her pulse pounding out a frantic beat at the base of her throat. Even though a cool breeze blew through the tower from the windows, cooling the warmth of summer, her palms were clammy.

It was five minutes before Cyrus was due to arrive when she heard the hoofbeats pounding on the grass. She'd been ready ages ago, and hadn't done much more than pace her living room, wringing her hands, distracted. When she heard the hooves, she took a deep breath and went to the balcony to watch him approach, waving.

He waved back from astride his horse, and she marvelled at the fact that he didn't fall off. What was it like to ride a horse? Was it easy, or difficult? Could she learn someday if she ever left this tower? How long did it take? She'd have to ask him what it was like. There was so much she wanted to ask him about the world and his experiences of it.

"Morning!" she called, when he was close enough to hear.

Reaching her, he dismounted and grinned, waving up at her again. "Morning."

It was a slightly cloudier day today, but still blue-skied, the sun occasionally blotted out by fluffy white clouds. Cyrus tied his horse to the same tree as usual and turned to her. The sun peeked out from behind a cloud, splashing across his brown hair and making it shine. It looked like he'd trimmed his beard.

"I have an idea!" she told him, before she could lose her nerve.

"You do? What might that be?"

"Well, I always wrap my hair when my mother comes by. She comes into the tower, and we eat together and talk, and it's never been dangerous…" She hitched in a breath and blustered on. She couldn't lose confidence now. She pointed to the silver silk wrap on her head. "I wrapped it today. And I cleaned the tower, top to bottom. I thought if I did, it couldn't hurt to have a guest."

"Which guest?" Cyrus said. He looked over his shoulder and cupped his hand over his brows, and it took her a moment to realise he was joking. "Who are you standing me up for?" he added, pretending to search the treeline.

She burst out laughing. "It's you, silly!"

He chortled. "I think it's a fine idea. I'd love to meet you properly. Shall I come to the door?"

"No," she said, "the door's locked. My mother has the key."

There was a long pause. "You don't have one of your own?" he asked.

"No. She thinks it's less tempting that way. Less dangerous."

"I… see." He sounded hesitant.

"You'd have to climb the ivy." She gestured to it, snaking up the pale purple brickwork of the tower in droves. "I know it's not exactly safe, but it's not too high up. I once tried to climb down it to get out…"

"You did?" Now his voice had an edge of amusement to it.

"When I was a child. There was a carnival happening in the town square. I could hear it from the tower and I felt left out. Gothel knew I'd be tempted. She was watching from the forest to make sure I didn't go. She stopped me before my feet touched the grass."

"That's a shame. I'm guessing it was the celebration of the goddess of light."

"It was."

"I've been a few times. The fireworks are wonderful."

"I could see some of them from my tower," Annice admitted, "but I missed out on everything else – the glowing fish in tanks, the plants they bring in, the dancers and the music. I think Gothel regretted giving me a book on the Kingdom of Lumen. It's where I read about the festival."

"Should you ever find a cure for your curse, I'll take you myself."

"That's…" She tried to formulate words and to ignore the pleasant buzzing in her head. He wanted to take her places. "It's kind of you."

"Right." He rubbed his hands together eagerly. "I best get climbing."

He gripped the ivy, lifting his foot onto the first hard vine and pulling himself up, grasping the next with his hand. She watched him ascend, worried he'd fall, her hand gripping her skirts. Nearby, his horse snuffled and tipped its nose up, as if wondering what its owner was doing.

Cyrus was soon almost at her balcony. He was nimble and quick, considering he was a bard and not an acrobat or circus performer. She stepped back when he drew level with her balcony, and he began to climb sideways with a few light grunts until finally, he dropped down, his boots hitting the stone balcony floor.

He turned to her, and she finally got to see him close up.

His brown hair was slightly golden, like it'd been exposed to the sun a few too many times, and fell down to brush his chin. He tucked a strand behind his ear and beamed at her. His sideburns were thick as honey. She hadn't been able to see his eye colour clearly when he'd been on the ground. Now a pair of crystalline blue eyes looked at her, reminding her of pictures she'd seen of the sea. Even his skin was sun-kissed. She wondered if he liked walking or lying on the beach, or just spending time in the meadows and hills of Lumen.

His clothes were covered in leaves from climbing the ivy and brushing past the flowers and shrubs lining the tower. He dusted a few off.

"Made it," he said. His eyes swept up and down, drinking her in, and she felt embarrassed, resisting the urge to shield her face with her hands.

Down below on the grass, the horse whickered. "Does your horse have a name? Will it be okay down there on its own?"

"His name is Max. He'll be fine. He likes his own company."

She smiled. "Riding must be such fun. I've always wanted to try."

"It can be. Max is well-trained so he doesn't throw me off like some other horses might. Bellamy's horse is a bit cheeky."

Annice nodded, wishing she had something more interesting to say or to contribute. "Do you want some tea?"

"I'd love some. Can I sit?" He gestured to the table and chairs positioned on her balcony, where there was a patch of warm sunlight.

"Go ahead."

He flopped down in a seat, the sun falling across his face and neck, and tipped his head back. Annice hurried inside to fetch some tea.

She was so nervous her hands shook, and after she'd boiled the water, it took her several attempts to pour tea into the pot with the tea leaves without spilling it everywhere. When she was done, she placed the pot and two cups onto a tray – adding some fruit at the last minute – and brought them out to him. In the living room, she had to stop to compose herself. Her hands were trembling and the teacups clinked together.

Calm down! she urged herself. *Stop being such a fool.* She didn't want to look weak or silly in front of him. Gripping the tray tightly, she made her way back onto the balcony and deposited the tray on the table. Cyrus had his eyes closed as he soaked up the sun's rays.

"Here you go," she said. "It's plain Lumen tea, I'm afraid. Nothing special."

He opened his eyes and sat forwards. "Thanks."

She took to her own seat opposite him. She was about to start pouring the tea when she noticed a shiny, dark-blue something inside one of the teacups.

"Oh, what's that?" she said, and leaned forwards, to see a small midnight-blue beetle shining in the cup.

"What?" Cyrus leaned forwards at the same time, close to her over the tabletop, and moved his hand to tilt the teacup towards him.

"A beetle, see? How did that get there? Maybe there's a hole in the cupboard."

It happened in an instant. As they were both leaning forwards to look at the unusual little creature, her hair wrap shifted on her head. Before she could grab it, a strand of hair fell out – part of her shorter fringe, which swept across the side of her face – and dropped straight onto Cyrus's hand.

Chapter Four

Spidery black lines sped across Cyrus's hand, bulging like veins, and he cried out in agony as the threads snaked towards his fingers, gradually turning the flesh black. Annice snatched the hair away and flew backwards so quickly she nearly toppled her seat. She staggered up and away from him, breathing hard, stuffing the strand back into the wrap. Cyrus was clutching the wrist of the hand she'd touched with her hair.

"I'm so sorry! Are you okay? Oh, lights, say something!"

"I'm... fine," he said. He managed a smile. "It grazed me."

Annice's heart was slamming against her chest. She looked down at his hand, but kept her distance. The spidery black lines were still bulging but the blackness was fading. She exhaled. The contact must have been too brief, but a few seconds longer… He could have ended up with a cursed hand to match the hair on her head. He would never have been able to ride Max again without killing the beast. And how would that have affected his work as a bard? His friendship with Bellamy? No inn would want to hire a troupe where the bard suffered from the curse of the rampion. And if any more of her hair had touched him… He could have died.

"I think you should go," Annice said shakily.

"Go?" he repeated. "We haven't even had our tea."

She'd been foolish to think she could bring him here. Gothel was always telling her it only took one mistake. She'd thought Cyrus would be safe because she was always so vigilant with Gothel. She'd been wrong. She'd let her guard down because she'd been so caught up in him, and so nervous.

"I'm sorry," she said weakly. "Please, could you go? We shouldn't have done this."

Cyrus lowered his injured hand and stood up slowly. He looked hurt, but quickly covered it up with a soft smile. "If that's what you want. No need to apologise. Can I at least come back again to talk? From down there, obviously." He motioned at the edge of the balcony.

Annice hesitated. She'd thought talking would be fine, but in the end, it had only tempted her to go one step further, to bring him up here. To take a risk. And look how that turned out. He was talented, and had so much of Nethervale to see and experience. If she ended up robbing him of that because of her hair… Gothel had been right. Risks weren't worth it and caution was everything.

"I don't know," she said. "I don't think it's a good idea."

"Well, no hard feelings. I'm disappointed I won't get to see you again but… I can respect your wishes, and I understand why."

He was taking it so well, so gallantly. She felt a surge of affection for him. She could see the hurt in his eyes, but he was smiling through it anyway.

"You can take some fruit with you," she said lamely, pointing at the grapes. She wanted to do something nice for him before he left, to make up for what she'd done. She hadn't even managed to pour him some tea.

He plucked a fat green grape and popped it in his mouth. "Best not take more. Max will want it, and he'll be bothering me all the way back to the town."

Her heart twanged at the mention of the horse. She wanted to carry on seeing him riding Max towards her across the meadow, but she knew it was for the best he didn't return.

"Well, it was very nice to meet you, Annice," he said. "Truly. I hope you don't give up on your music. And I'll listen out for it, whenever I'm riding by."

"I'll make sure I keep playing, then," she said, swallowing down the lump in her throat. She stepped aside into the doorway of her tower, so he could climb back down the ivy.

Her heart sank another few inches when he clambered onto the balcony's side and gripped the ivy, making his way down.

"Goodbye," he called to her, with one last glance over his shoulder before he turned away.

"Bye, Cyrus," she called back.

She watched him untie Max and ride away across the bright green fields, the grass rippling around them both. He didn't look back again.

Over the next week, Annice did nothing but mope around her tower. She tried to distract herself with music as she'd promised Cyrus she wouldn't give up on it, but it was hard to focus. She kept thinking of the dark veins bursting across his hand, and felt sick at the thought that she could have killed someone. How would she have been able to live with herself?

Gothel had noticed something was wrong. She'd been asking Annice what was the matter, but Annice had so far used the excuse that she hadn't been sleeping in the summer warmth. Just over a week later, they were having lunch on the balcony as per their usual summertime routine. Gothel had brought a tomato and basil pasta dish from a new restaurant that had opened in town. It smelt divine, but Annice could only pick at it, the bowl sitting in her lap. She twirled the strings of spaghetti and tomato sauce around her fork and sighed.

"Right," Gothel said, setting down her own dish with a clank. She'd already finished hers and the bowl now only contained flecks of herbs and leftover sauce. "Are you going to tell me what's really the matter?" she demanded. "I don't believe this 'I'm tired' nonsense. You aren't yourself and there's more to it. I'm not a fool. I brought you some new books last week and you haven't even touched them. And I know one of them was one you were excited to read."

Annice gave a one-shouldered shrug. Telling the truth would mean admitting that she'd allowed herself to get close to Cyrus, that she'd invited him up here and nearly killed him. But she had to give Gothel something.

"I'm twenty-one now," she started. She supposed she could tell a half-truth. "I'm tired of not having any friends, or someone to court and start a life with. It's lonely up here in the tower." Gothel opened her mouth to continue but Annice held up her hand to stop her. "I know you come by all the time. But it isn't the same. Surely you realise? I need… friendships, and something more. I want to be around people my own age. I don't even know what that feels like. I want to meet people who share my interests…" She didn't add that she'd already met two people who liked music. "I can't go on like this up here."

Gothel heaved a sigh and folded her hands into her lap. "I know. Someday, this will all be over, and you'll have a normal life. You have to be patient."

How many years had Gothel been saying the same thing? Annice had been waiting since childhood. Nothing had changed. How many more years would she have to wait? And what if they never found a cure?

"Friends are out there, waiting for you," Gothel went on. "They'll still be there when we find a cure."

Annice nodded lamely, but she didn't really agree. No one was going to wait for her; hardly anyone knew she was here. Her mind was swinging a different way now. Didn't she *have* a friend already, in Cyrus? They hadn't known each other long but she was sure she could describe him as a friend. If she waited for a cure, it could be decades from now. How would she feel twenty years in the future, if she'd let that go? If she was still alone? And when Gothel died, who would she have left? Nobody. She'd be completely alone, especially if she disregarded Cyrus. She didn't want that. Just the thought of it made her heart ache and her stomach swirl.

"What about when you're gone?" she pressed Gothel, glancing up at her. Gothel paled and opened her mouth to speak again, but Annice rushed on. "It's going to happen one day. You're older than me. Who would bring me food? How would I survive? I'd have no choice but to leave the tower, then. And I wouldn't even be equipped to deal with the world outside." The words tumbled out, and each one felt like an icicle stabbing into her chest. She'd thought about this often, in the small hours of the night, and she'd tried to talk to Gothel about it frequently. Her fears were always pushed to the side.

"Not this again." Gothel pressed two fingertips to her forehead, frowning. "You're thinking too far in the future—"

"You always say that!" Annice cried. She slammed her bowl onto the table and stood up. She was tired of having her concerns brushed away like dust. Like they were unimportant. "It's a genuine concern, Mother! Something we have to think about! But you always refuse to listen to me. You can't keep me safe forever. One day you won't be here, and you have to help me prepare."

"Help you *how*?" Gothel said shortly, standing up as well. Her mouth was turned down. "You want me to start letting you leave, putting every other living thing at risk? So you can feel comfortable about what happens twenty years from now?"

Annice pursed her lips. Gothel was twisting her words again. It was infuriating. She balled her hands into fists, trying to keep her temper.

"That's not what I meant," she ground out.

"Then what, Annice? What do you expect of me?"

"This is pointless. You never listen."

"Yes, it is pointless." Gothel began gathering up the dishes and made her way back through the tower door, towards the kitchen. Her every word dripped with bitterness. "You know I'm right. We'll deal with what to do when I'm dead once I'm frail and struggling. As of yet, I'm not."

She swept away, leaving Annice standing on the balcony, shaking with fury.

———

Annice and her mother's goodbye was colder than usual, once all the lunch things had been cleared away. Gothel pressed a kiss to her cheek, but Annice didn't reciprocate.

"I'll see you the day after tomorrow," said Gothel.

Annice nodded but said nothing. Gothel left the tower with her basket over her arm, skirts swishing behind her.

When she was gone, Annice stewed in her bad mood. Previously, she'd felt guilty for hiding Cyrus from Gothel – now she felt it might be for the best.

Her thoughts turned to Cyrus again. Gothel was wrong; the world wasn't waiting for Annice, and it wouldn't wait for her to find a cure. The world was happening out there, right now. And Cyrus was part of it. He'd noticed her. He felt like the first genuine friend she'd had. Maybe it wouldn't be so bad, to keep him as a friend, and hope for nothing more? He could come and talk to her, and listen to her music.

She rushed over to her writing desk and penned a letter furiously.

Dear Cyrus,

I'm sorry for what happened, and I was wrong to say we shouldn't see each other again. We have things in common, and I want to hear your stories about the rest of Nethervale, and kingdoms I haven't been able to see. I want to see you again. But only from a distance. I can't invite you inside the tower again. Putting you in danger is the last thing I want to do.

I understand if you can't agree, but I'd love it if you did. Perhaps you could even bring Bellamy, and we could all talk. I'd like to know more about you both.

Yours,
Annice

She had to wait for the daily newspaper to arrive with the bluebird messenger before she could send the letter on its way. When it came, she clamped the letter in the tiny bird's beak, and hoped desperately that Cyrus would reply.

Annice tried to keep herself busy, but she didn't need to wait long. The reply came within days – and too close to one of Gothel's visits for her liking. Gothel had only just left when the tiny bluebird dropped itself onto the balcony and twittered at her.

She grabbed the letter from its beak and tore it open, devouring the words hungrily.

He wanted to see her again! He'd even suggested a day, two days from now. And his final line read *I'm glad you wrote to me again*.

On Gothel's next visit, Annice told her she wanted the full day to spend on her music on the day Cyrus was coming, so she wouldn't come. Gothel looked surprised; Annice had never asked her to stay at home before.

"If you wish," she said stiffly. "I know you're having a difficult time, Annice, but I hope you won't let it affect our relationship. I only want to protect you."

"I *know*," Annice said. She tried to make herself sound bright. It wasn't difficult; all she had to do was think about Cyrus. "It isn't you. Really. I just want to be serious about finishing this piece of music and I need all day to focus. I've enjoyed doing that, when you've been on your dates."

That seemed to convince her.

The day Cyrus finally returned, Annice cleaned the tower, top to bottom, as usual. She wrapped her hair – avoiding the silky, silver wrap she'd used last time, just in case, and instead opting for a purple one. The dress she chose was deep blue, with a slightly dipped V in the chest, where she hung a silver moon pendant.

She didn't wait on the balcony this time but sat reading one of her new books, her stomach fluttering with nervous anticipation. When she heard the hooves, she went out to greet him, waving down at him and grinning.

After he'd dismounted and tied Max to a tree, she studied him. His clothes were all black today, and looser than his usual attire, the top buttons of his shirt undone so she could see the sun-kissed skin of his chest. That caused even more chaos in her stomach, and she swallowed. He'd tied his hair into a short ponytail, showing off the angles of his jaw. She wished she could run her fingers across it, trace every bone and every curve and see what it would be like to touch a man. His hand seemed better, but it was difficult to tell from here.

"Are you alright?" she called. "Your hand?"

"I'm fine," he said, wiggling it at her. "No damage done. It's back to normal."

Annice exhaled. "Good. No Bellamy?" She'd meant it when she said he could bring his friend.

"He had a bit too much mead after our performance last night – he was flirting with another young man afterwards, and got carried away." Cyrus laughed. "I'm glad you asked me to come back."

Her heart jumped. "Me too."

"What changed your mind?"

"Something my mother said. She doesn't know about you; she wouldn't like it if she found out you were here. But she was telling me there would be friends waiting for me when I leave the tower, and I realised I'd already found one."

He hesitated for so long she wondered if he were

going to reply at all. Eventually, he said, "Does she think you'll be able to leave one day?"

"We both hope so. She's visited all the apothecaries in the Kingdom of Lumen but they don't know anything about a cure for the rampion curse. She's written to overseas apothecaries, but they're not much more help. Some of them don't even respond. She's saving up to travel, to see if there's anything she can find out. But travel is expensive."

"It doesn't have to be," said Cyrus. He sounded doubtful, and pushed a hand into one of his pockets. "It's more time-consuming than expensive, honestly. We didn't have much when we left our home. We exchanged work for passage – entertaining the sailors with our music. I've heard of other people offering to clean, help out on the deck, cook. It's quite common when you have little money."

Annice frowned. "You can really do that?"

"If you find the right ship, yes."

Why had Gothel never mentioned that? Had she ever considered it as an option? She had skills in herbs and botany and knew remedies and tinctures. She wasn't a bad cook, either. It wouldn't be hard for her to offer work for passage. A cold feeling seeped into Annice's heart.

"You didn't know?" Cyrus asked.

"No." The cold feeling intensified.

They were silent for several minutes. Cyrus was the

one to break it: "You've never tried to leave the tower, all these years?"

"I've tried to help myself. I wanted to write to people who could help me – apothecaries, librarians, professors – but Gothel would never give me any addresses. She always did it herself. She said it was too stressful for me to handle. She never wavered, even though I had all the time in the world." Annice paused. "I tried to escape once as a child. I broke my arm climbing out of the tower. And I didn't wrap my hair then. All the grass around me died when I hit the ground and it scared me. I felt horrible. I stopped trying after that. I didn't want to hurt anyone – or anything – else."

"You could try writing to some of those apothecaries overseas yourself now," he suggested. "If you want to keep on trying now. There are no guarantees, but it's worth a try, isn't it? Maybe things have changed since your mother wrote to them. There are always new discoveries going on. Someone might have discovered something new."

"Thank you, that's a good point. I doubt Gothel would like the idea, though. She's so overprotective. Do you think you'd be able to get some addresses for me, of overseas apothecaries?"

"Consider it done." He gave a low bow, looked up at her and grinned.

"Just like that?"

"Of course. It's like you said. We're friends."

Something turned over inside of her. *I wish we could*

be more, she thought sadly. She wanted to know what it would be like, if he took her hand in his. If he wrapped his arms around her. If his hair fell across her bare skin. What would it be like to have him court her? Take her out for wine and to restaurants? Annice would never know and it stung.

He must have detected something was amiss – in her posture, or her face – because he said, "Are you okay?"

"I'm fine," she whispered, and had to repeat it because he wouldn't have heard. She raised her voice. "I just wish my mother wasn't so overbearing. That she'd let me have some freedoms, even small ones."

He looked about the meadow, at the softly shifting grass moving in the breeze and the daisies swaying. "My family weren't always the nicest people, either."

"Really?"

"Yes. I always hoped to find a better one, out there somewhere. To build my own, have some stability."

"You want to have a family?" she said. Family was important to her, too. She had Gothel, but whenever she read her novels, she dreamed of what it'd be like to build a family with someone else. It didn't even necessarily have to involve children – she wasn't sure how she felt on that subject yet. But someone who loved her, maybe a pet or two – cats, she'd prefer – and shared interests, dreams they could build on together. That was family as she wanted it. "What kind of family would you have?" she asked Cyrus.

"Someone to love and care for. To experience life with, travel with. I came close once," he said. "Or I thought I did. At home, I loved someone. But she wanted to stay in one place. She didn't want to travel Nethervale, like I did. She married someone else and here I am."

She wanted to stay in one place. The words struck Annice like bricks. She'd always wanted to travel, to see everything Nethervale had to offer – every piece of land, every kingdom, every touch of wonder. But she was stuck in one place through no fault of her own. It was another reason they were better off as friends, when she couldn't give him what he wanted.

"I'm sure you'll find someone who can travel with you," Annice said. She tried to sound encouraging but it was hard with the lump in her throat.

"It's hard, when I move around so often, to get to know people. It's been refreshing, talking with you here. There are no distractions, like mead or music or loud drunk people."

Annice laughed. "Sounds like it could be fun, though." She'd always wanted to experience a party; the wild tavern experience she often read about. Another item on the list of things she hoped to do.

"It can be," he agreed. "But sometimes you want something deeper, you know? Even if we stay in one place long enough to make friends, we move on again, and then it all goes away. It's difficult to put down roots when you're always travelling, but it's what we do, and we love it." He laughed and raked a hand through his hair. "I'm sorry. I'm rambling."

"Ramble away. I really don't mind."

They were more similar than she'd thought. He was out in the world but he still sounded lonely. She'd never imagined a life outside the tower, travelling Nethervale, could be that way.

"What if you had a travelling family?" she asked him. "Someone you loved who would come with you. Maybe a few dogs."

"I'd love that," he said, his face splitting into a wide grin. "I've always wanted to get a small caravan instead of travelling everywhere on horseback and staying in the inns we play at. Turn it into a small home."

"A travelling home. Sounds wonderful."

She could imagine it. A red-painted caravan, with yellow flowers on the side, and huge spoked wheels, pulled by two horses who looked like Max, except they had black patches instead of sand-coloured ones. Inside there would be room for a small blanket-laden bed, a seating area, a tiny kitchen stocked with utensils for cooking on the road over open fires. It would be cramped and quirky and cosy, nothing like her tower.

Annice pushed the images away. She couldn't be the one who went with him, as much as her heart ached for that kind of life.

They continued to talk for hours, moving away from the subject of what they wanted from life and onto simpler things. He told her stories about all the places he'd visited and she marvelled at his descriptions of cities filled with marble buildings, tiny villages with sloping rooftops, vast marshy plains filled with swaying white plants, and dolphins leaping through the water beside ships.

When it was time for him to go and he'd untied Max, the sun was sinking towards the treetops, turning the sky purple. Luckily, he'd brought a waterskin, and he'd shaded himself under the tree Max was tied to while they talked, otherwise he might have dehydrated or burnt in the sun. She couldn't believe they'd talked for so long. Her throat was hoarse and scratchy despite the fact that she'd gone inside to fetch a pitcher of apple juice.

"I'll write you," Cyrus said, as he tucked his waterskin away and clambered onto Max, pushing his feet into the stirrups.

"I'll be waiting," she said, smiling. "We can arrange a day for you to come again."

"I'd like that. Take care, Annice."

She waved him off. This time he turned when he was halfway across the meadow and waved back; she was surprised he didn't fall off Max. A laugh escaped her and she clamped her hands to her cheeks, watching as he vanished into the trees.

Chapter Five

Cyrus was true to his word. He'd soon written to
her again, and he'd enclosed addresses for apothecaries across Nethervale – dozens of the most
well-respected and renowned ones, one of which was
even an expert working at the University of Botany,
Healing and Apothecarial Studies. Annice made sure
to keep the letters hidden from Gothel, keeping them
stowed away in one of the drawers beside her bed,
underneath her hair wraps.

She wrote to them one by one over the coming days.
It wasn't something she was comfortable with entirely –
she felt like she was deceiving Gothel, who had already
tried this method – but she kept reminding herself it
couldn't do any harm. Each letter went the same way,
with only the name of the apothecary amended:

My name is Annice and I come from the King-dom of Lumen. It's a place of light and we're known for our unusual glowing plants. Or so I'm told. They don't grow around my home, and I can't go to see them, because I'm trapped here.

When I was a child, I encountered the rampion flower, and now my hair is cursed. I'm sure you know what that means already, being an expert. I have no life of my own. I rely on someone else to bring me food. I can't leave here. I recently turned twenty-one and all I want is to travel, have ad-ventures, find love and do everything else afforded to other people my age. I want to have a real life before I grow old and die. I can't spend the rest of my life trapped behind closed doors.

Please, if you know anything about the rampion's curse, or possible treatments, I'd love to hear from you. I have little money, and in my situation, cannot travel the entirety of Nethervale for answers, but I can send you valuables – I do own some jewellery – in exchange for information.

Yours,
Annice

She sealed each letter with red wax, and when the bluebird came back with the newspaper, held them up to him. He tipped his head to one side, chirruped and flew away. He'd be back, though. This number of letters was too thick to clutch in his beak as a parcel, so he would return with a carry case.

When the letters were finally sent off, Annice watched the bluebird depart, her throat tight and thick with nerves. Would she get any responses? And would they bring her any hope?

———⟨ᴗᴗᴗ⟩———

No responses had come after a few days, but Annice had expected that, since the letters would have to be taken overseas, and it would take more time than if she were writing to someone in the Kingdom of Lumen. She kept herself occupied with both Gothel and Cyrus's visits. Cyrus came back several more times – Annice made sure it was always on the days where Gothel would be absent. The more time she spent with Cyrus, the more she found herself feeling as though she were floating around her tower, airy-headed and light. She accidentally smashed a dish because she wasn't paying attention one morning, and on another day, she almost overflowed her bath because she'd been daydreaming about Cyrus.

On Gothel's next visit, it was raining, so the tower shutters were closed across the window, the droplets banging against the wood. Candles and lamps were lit across the sitting room. Annice was sitting with her bare feet drawn up on the loveseat, already in her nightdress. Gothel had stayed much later than usual because she was telling Annice about work at the flower shop, and they'd ended up drinking wine together.

"Dathan is a very infuriating man," Gothel said, from her position sitting on the rug across from Annice. She was complaining about the man who did deliveries for her flower shop and helped her with the day-to-day work. "He's always making mistakes. I should replace him. He's useless."

There was a table between them with the wine bottle and goblets perched on top. There was also a bowl of garlic breadsticks for snacks; they'd already demolished a pasta dish earlier, the dirty plates now resting in the sink.

Annice's head was light from the wine, and she felt giggly, as if a silly word would drop out of her mouth any moment. She tried hard to restrain herself from talking about Cyrus. Maybe the wine hadn't been a good idea? But they were enjoying themselves, and she felt content.

"I'm sure he's trying his best," said Annice.

"Bah," Gothel growled. "I need a partner, someone I can rely on at the shop. Not a fool."

Annice thought of Cyrus, and his dreams of travelling with someone he loved, a family and a home on the road. It aligned with her own dreams for the future. "It's good to have shared visions in a partnership."

Gothel lifted a grey eyebrow. "How very mature of you."

Annice snickered, grabbing her goblet and glugging some more wine.

"I suppose it's all those books you read, teaching you strong lessons about love. I'm glad you're so mature, my darling."

"Oh, it's not *just* the books!" Annice blurted, and fell about laughing.

"What else could it be?" Gothel asked, her hand freezing halfway to her own goblet.

"Nothing." Annice flapped a hand to dismiss her, but nearly sloshed wine onto her nightdress – not a good idea, since it was white, but her hands seemed to have a mind of their own. "I… I daydream a lot!"

"The bluebird messenger has been coming here a lot recently."

Annice stilled, gripping her goblet.

"Who would you be writing so many letters to?" Gothel pressed.

"I…" Annice scrambled for words, but her mind was muzzy. She'd been about to mention the apothecaries, but she didn't want Gothel to know about that, either. She wanted answers of her own, without Gothel's involvement. She was starting to distrust her, as if she wasn't trying hard enough to figure out an answer to the curse. Annice wanted to be in control of her own life. The best thing she could come up with was, "No one. I mean, the seamstress."

"The seamstress."

"Yes. I wanted to ask about a new dress."

"But you always do that through me. You never write her directly unless there's a problem with a purchase." Gothel was standing up now, smoothing down her dress and glancing across the room at the writing desk. "Are you lying to me about something, Annice?"

"What? No! Why would you think that? It's ridiculous." The words tumbled out too quickly, like spilled marbles. Annice knew she sounded defensive, and wished she could take the words back and try again. She tried to scramble up from the sofa and tripped, almost crashing into the table and catching herself at the last minute. "Please, Mother, sit down. Have some more wine."

"You're hiding something from me. I overlooked it at first. I thought you might be sending off shopping orders, or doing something with your writing I didn't know about."

"I… I am! It was shopping! And…" She trailed off, trying to come up with something involving her writing that would sound genuine, but the wine had fuzzed her sense of logic and all she could do was gape at Gothel in disbelief.

Gothel swept to the writing desk, rummaging through the small drawer and the scattered papers.

"Gothel, stop!" Annice cried. "There's nothing there!" Thank goodness she'd hidden her letters from Cyrus in the bedroom. "*See?*" she hissed when Gothel was done. "Sit down! Tell me more about Dathan!"

But Gothel wasn't done. She swept across the room and began tearing Annice's books from the shelves.

"What are you doing?" Annice screeched. "Be careful with them!"

Book after book was flung onto the floor, as if Gothel expected letters to be slipped behind them, out of view. An old, battered hardback landed roughly on its spine and split. Annice gave a wordless cry and made to grab Gothel's arm, but her mother was surprisingly strong. She grappled with Annice and shoved her away, so she fell back onto the loveseat.

"I *will* find what you're hiding, Annice!" Gothel snapped. "Don't try to stop me. It's pointless. Do you want to end up hurting me?"

Annice realised her wrap was loosening and gave a moan. She could have harmed Gothel, just like she had Cyrus. She raced into the bathroom to fix it, while Gothel kept ripping apart the sitting room, searching for something incriminating.

When Annice came back, Gothel had already been through her bedroom. She was standing on the sitting room rug, facing Annice, a wad of letters gripped in her hand. She was scowling. Behind her, the shutters clattered as rain slammed against them.

"What," Gothel ground out, "are *these*?"

"Give them back, please!" Annice ran at her, making a grab for the letters, but Gothel was taller, and held them out of reach, stepping back towards the window.

"Watch yourself!" Gothel cried.

Annice froze and then jerked backwards. She'd just fixed her hair wrap. She didn't want it to loosen again, risking Gothel's wellbeing. But she *needed* those letters.

"Please," she breathed.

Gothel strode to the writing desk and spread some of the letters out on the wood, picking out lines, her voice shaking with rage. "*Dear Annice, it was lovely to see you again today… Dear Annice, I haven't laughed that much in ages… Dear Annice, we have some shows but I'll come back in a few days…*" She continued reading line after line, and heat bloomed across Annice's face. She felt ashamed, like she'd done something wrong, when all she'd done was make a connection with someone she liked, who liked her back. The realisation made anger spread through her, quick as rushing water.

"Don't look at me like that!" she shouted at Gothel. "I'm entitled to have a life, like you!"

"A *life*?" Gothel snatched up the letters again and waved them in the air, squeezing them so tightly they crumpled. "This isn't a life, Annice, this is *dangerous*. You're putting this man at risk, and for what? What do you hope to accomplish? *Love*?" She sneered. Annice had never seen such a hateful look on her face. "You know you can never have that."

Annice's breath caught in her chest. Pain lanced through her. "Never?" she breathed. "You're always telling me we'll figure something out!"

Gothel's features remained hard. She began gathering up her things, dumping the letters in the basket she'd brought, and snatched up her midnight-blue cloak from the hook on the wall, spreading it over her shoulders.

"You foolish girl," she said. "It doesn't matter what we've said or haven't said. Only your actions matter right now, and you've acted like a child and failed to listen to me."

It wasn't cold in the sitting room, but goosebumps sprang up over Annice's arms, and she pulled her sleeves down. Was Gothel right? Had all of this been a bad idea? She thought back to the black thread marks spreading across Cyrus's skin, how his hand had seized up. They'd talked about it in their letters. When Gothel saw that in black ink, she'd know what Annice had done, and how she'd invited him up here.

"I'm leaving now," Gothel barked. "You can have the rest of the wine."

"W-What are you going to do?" Annice said.

"Go through these letters for a start. Write to this Cyrus and tell him he can't see you anymore. And sort out some precautions so this never happens again."

"Precautions?" What did *that* mean? When Gothel didn't answer and only pulled up her hood, Annice said, "What precautions?"

She didn't respond. Instead, she swept past Annice and down the staircase. Annice heard the tower door slam as she left, and the clunk of the key turning in the lock.

———✿✿✿———

Annice drank the rest of the wine before bed; it was the only way she could sleep. When she woke, she was groggy and had a headache pulsing across her forehead. She'd never drunk enough wine to feel ill before. She wrapped her hair, made herself a pitcher of water, and pressed a cold cloth to her forehead. She couldn't bring herself to clean, but the tower had been cleaned yesterday, so she was sure it was fine. Only her room was at risk of hairs being present and her hair was firmly wrapped. She felt sick when she thought about what had happened yesterday, and the way Gothel had looked before stalking out of the tower.

Gothel didn't stop by all day. Annice started to panic. Had she abandoned her for a time, to punish her? Or was she meeting with Dathan about deliveries? She couldn't remember if Gothel had mentioned having work today.

Padding over to her writing desk, her heart nearly stopped. All her writing materials were gone. The papers, her pens, stamps, her wax seal. Nothing remained except scraps of discarded letters she hadn't sent, and an empty inkpot.

Hands shaking, Annice went back to the loveseat. She couldn't even write Cyrus to tell him what had happened. She couldn't write to Gothel to ask when she was coming back. She'd taken her means of communication.

Taking some deep breaths, she tried to calm herself. Gothel wouldn't abandon her; it was a silly notion.

Gothel would be back soon, when she'd calmed down. She'd give her the letter-writing utensils eventually.

Annice waited two days, and Gothel didn't return. Annice's cupboards were beginning to look bare. She was frightened she'd run out of food. And when she opened the shutters on the tower the second morning, she stilled. She'd heard someone cough down below, by the door.

"Gothel?" she called down, craning over the balcony to try to see her. The grass was wet with a fine drizzle of morning rain and the sky was a patchwork of clouds. "Is that you?"

A man clomped into view, and Annice's heart leapt into her throat, where it pulsed. He was wearing silver-plated armour, similar to the type the Royal Guard wore – she'd seen them pass her tower before in the distance. At his waist was a heavyset sword, far longer and thicker than the one Cyrus carried. His shoulders were wide, his head beefy, and he peered up at her with crossed, muscular arms.

"No, ma'am, not Gothel," he said. Despite the politeness of his words, he sounded harsh, gravelly. "But she did send me."

"What? Why? What do you want?"

"Want? I don't want anything, except my coin. She's paid me to guard this tower, so that's what I'm doing. Told me you're a danger to yourself and others, or something."

For a moment, Annice couldn't make any more words come out. *Paid* him? Gothel had always been frugal to try to save for her trip abroad to visit more apothecaries and experts. It was why Annice got so many books from the library, rather than new ones – and when she did get new ones for her bookshelves, they were typically old library stock anyway. Gothel made most of Annice's hair wraps and dresses from fabric she could buy more cheaply, except on special occasions, like her birthday.

Yet she'd hired a guard. And she'd told him Annice was a danger to... herself? It didn't make sense. Annice could admit she was a danger to others, but herself? Why was Gothel presenting her that way? Anger prickled at her skin.

"How much is she paying you?" Annice demanded. "How long are you supposed to stay?"

The man seemed to puff up, looking proud of himself. "She's paying me far better than my last job guarding some nobleman's manor house. She said it could be indefinite. Who knows? I'm happy to stay for that amount of coin."

Annice was unable to respond. Words had left her. The man waited a while for her to reply, then gave up and returned to his post – probably by the tower door, given the direction he'd moved. He was out of sight again.

She turned slowly, as though moving through slush, and went inside. For five long minutes she stood in the middle of her sitting room, staring at nothing, thinking.

Although she'd been stuck here since she was a child, she'd never truly felt like a prisoner, least of all *Gothel's* prisoner. She was her mother. She was doing what she felt was right. Annice's hair was dangerous and could do damage, so it was only right she should be shut away.

Wasn't it?

Her mind whirred. That's what she'd always believed, but now she felt like some lies were unspooling. Gothel had money, more money than she'd allowed Annice to believe. Come to think of it, she was always going on work trips. To restaurants, inns, wineries, botanical gardens. Annice had assumed Dathan was helping to pay – or that Gothel had funding from somewhere else, because it was for work. Now she wasn't sure.

Cyrus. Had Gothel already told him to stay away? He might never come back. He'd never see the guard outside, or see what a mess she was in.

She gripped her skirt tightly, fingers shaking. This wasn't right; she knew it in her bones and in her heart. There were enough stories on her shelves about manipulation and psychological games. She'd been so hesitant to push Gothel before, to even push herself to take risks. But this was going too far. Having someone guard her tower was wrong, all wrong. Cutting her off from Cyrus was, too. She was allowed to build *some* semblance of a life from her tower – and Gothel wouldn't take that away from her. Even if she was her mother.

But how could she get to Cyrus, tell him what had happened?

An idea struck. She'd have to wait until darkness fell.

The guard had to sleep sometime.

⁓⁓⁓

She crouched in the shadows of the balcony, her hair already fully wrapped – as tightly as she could manage without a headache – and with a pouch of belongings hanging from her back. A little food and water. She remembered the name of the inn he was staying at, but didn't know how far away it was, so she might need it.

It was past midnight when she heard the deep, re-verberating snores. She waited a few more minutes to be sure he wouldn't wake up, then clambered onto the side of the balcony, gripping the tough, winding ivy running over the side of the tower.

The height of the tower had never bothered her before, but now, with the wind whistling around her neck and the grass far below, she felt dizzy. She swal-lowed. It wasn't *that* high; when Cyrus came to visit, she could see his face clearly. *I can do this.*

Slowly, and with care, she pushed her foot onto a lower branch of ivy, making her way down. She hoped Cyrus hadn't weakened it the last time he climbed.

Her hand nearly missed the next tangle and she squealed, snatching for another one and ending up at an awkward angle, her arm stretched unnaturally. She glanced over her shoulder – a bad idea. The grass looked like it might rise up to meet her.

Breathe.

She inhaled deeply through her nose and continued down.

When her flat shoes finally touched the bottom, she pushed out a huge sigh of relief and took a moment to steady herself. The guard was still snoring around the side of the tower. The snores were the only sound aside from the occasional hoot of an owl in the forest.

She remembered Cyrus's words about dangerous creatures. But there were none in this forest that she knew of – just deer, foxes and birds. Still, the trees across the grass looked menacing in a way she'd never noticed before. The swaying grass vanished into a mouthful of darkness, spitting bracken and dried twigs. Annice steeled herself. She'd never been afraid of the night and she wasn't about to start now.

She pressed on, into the trees, crossing into the gloom. Annice had barely made it ten paces further into the forest when her feet caught on something and an awful clanging sound rattled and filled the forest.

Gasping, she glanced down – and found her feet tangled in arranged strings, each hung with pots and pans and other utensils. A trap.

Scrabbling to get away, she turned, but only became more ensnared. She tripped and ended up on her backside in the dirt, grabbing at her ankles, trying to free them of the string.

Pounding footsteps nearby and the rattling of armour told her she was too late.

The guard snatched her up roughly by the arm until she was standing, bandy-legged, like a baby deer. She yelped – his grip was vicelike.

"You're hurting me! Let go!" she demanded, struggling and clawing at him. Atop her head, the hair wrap felt looser.

"You're not to leave the tower, girl." She could feel his warm breath on her face, and was all too aware of his closeness to her hair wrap. How much had Gothel told him about her curse, and the rampion? Did he know *anything*? He was a fool to get so close. He wouldn't come near Annice if he knew the truth. Why hadn't Gothel told him?

"How can you be so callous?" she cried. "You don't know anything! You don't know me, or Gothel! You're a stranger! Get away from me now, for your own good. I—"

"A stranger who is getting paid, and that's bloody well enough for me!" he barked, talking over her. There was a *shink* sound, and he bent down, cutting through the strings around her ankles with a knife. Terrified he might use it to threaten her next, she wriggled, trying to get free of his grasp.

"Leave me alone or you'll be killed by—" she started.

"Stop *moving*!" he barked, straightening and brandishing his knife.

She flinched away from the knife and flung out her hands, scrabbling at him, trying to push him away. He'd raised the blade as he straightened, and perhaps he hadn't intended to harm her, but her reaction was instinctive. She'd never been so close to a weapon before.

"I said—"

He never got to complete the sentence. Her hair wrap unravelled, spooling about her shoulders like a wreath of darkness. She screamed at him to get away from her, trying to move her hands, to pull her hair away from him. But his hand was still clenched around her upper arm, and a thick strand of hair fell across his wrist – then another, until all of her hair was freed, spilling over his skin. Her hair wrap fluttered to the ground in their struggle.

The reaction was immediate. Threads of shadow sprang across his skin, moving far quicker than the ones she'd seen on Cyrus's hand. In his fear, he only clutched at her tighter, and she couldn't pry herself free. The curse was given more time to spread. He wouldn't listen to her screams. The black veins moved up his arm, whizzing beneath his armour. They made their way to his face, stretching across his cheeks, crawling to his eyes.

"You little *bitch*, what did you do to me!" he shrilled.

The whites of his eyes blackened as the curse took hold. His body seized. She was sure her arm was going to bruise as she scrambled to get away, but he had a tight hold of her. Her voice cracked, her throat raw from yelling at him to stop.

Finally, he let go. Rigid, he fell backwards into a patch of moonlight. She could see the full effect of the curse. Black eyes. Crumbling, papery skin filling up with dark magic. Annice had to look away. When she looked back, he was nothing more than a patch of lifeless ash on the ground, disintegrated by her curse. Only the armour and the rest of his clothing remained.

Chapter Six

Annice's stomach hurt. She gripped it as she turned away, trying hard not to be sick, pulling in gulps of fresh air. She'd killed the guard. She hadn't meant to, but she had.

It could have been Cyrus.

By the time she was out on the grass again, tower back in sight, she was sobbing. Her hair was trailing behind her, killing all the grass and plants, making everything shrivel and die. She scrambled back up the ivy on the side of the tower, less careful this time. Some of the ivy blackened as she climbed, adding to the trail of death and destruction she'd left on her return. She'd deserve it, if the ivy gave out before she reached the top. Her legs and hands caught on some of the thorns positioned here and there, drawing blood. But she didn't care. She deserved the pain.

The ivy held out long enough for her to reach the top; she mustn't have brushed against it as much as she'd thought. It was a monumental effort to haul herself over the balcony when she reached it. When she did, she collapsed in a heap on the stone floor, almost banging her head on the outdoor chair. Her hair splayed around her, a dark cage, and her hands stung with cuts. More tears spilled free. She should have stayed here in the first place. Annice looked up at the milky moon, full and bulbous and surrounded by scatterings of stars. She'd killed someone. She'd live with the guilt forever.

She'd been so stupid, so childish. All her talk of taking risks and being less cautious, and for what? A man was dead. Did he have a partner at home, a wife or husband, family? Children? Pets, even? Someone must be waiting for him. They'd worry when he didn't come back. The worry would stretch on. They'd never know what happened to him, and it would crush them. She'd damaged more than one person tonight; she was sure of it. He might have been rough with her, but he'd been paid to do a job, that was all. He hadn't deserved to die.

She rolled onto her side, pressing her palms into her eyes to try to stem the tears. But they kept coming.

Annice wanted to rip every strand of hair from her head, but it'd accomplish nothing. The curse would ensure they grew back quickly.

She wasn't only trapped in the tower. Her body was a trap she couldn't escape from too. It was the first time that had occurred to her.

Fresh sobs burst forth, and this time she didn't try to stop them. She hunched in a ball on the stone, clutching her painful stomach and picturing the man turning to ash, over and over.

———

Annice couldn't hide her despair from Gothel, who did return a few days later with supplies to stock up Annice's kitchen. Annice had barely spoken to her when she stepped into the tower. She'd been wrapping her hair and cleaning every day even though she hadn't known when Gothel would come back, partly out of paranoia after what happened. She'd scrubbed the wood floors so hard her hands were red and blistered on top of the cuts from the thorns. As Gothel was dumping fresh fruit and vegetables onto the counter in a heap, she glanced over at Annice, who was sitting on the loveseat, stoic.

"You haven't said a word to me," Gothel said. "But it isn't because you're angry, is it?"

Annice's throat was as dry as sand. She hadn't had anything to drink all morning. And she'd expected this confrontation. Gothel would know something had happened. The scene outside was enough to show her the truth.

"I saw the guard's armour on the edge of the woods," Gothel continued snippily. "And all the dead plants you left behind you. I presume it was your doing?"

Her tone was harsh. It only added to the guilt that had been climbing inside Annice over the past day or so, clawing its way up her insides like a monster. Gothel's words made it tear free, and Annice burst into tears, fat droplets spilling over her cheeks.

She could barely see through her tears, but a moment later Gothel was sinking onto the loveseat beside her and taking her hand, grasping it tightly.

"Don't cry, child," she said, softer now at the sight of her daughter crying. "I knew we'd have… teething problems, when you reached a certain age. That you'd find it harder. I expected it sooner, especially when you started reading adventure novels!" Gothel gave her hand another squeeze and laughed.

Annice smiled and gulped back a sob, wiping at her cheeks with the long sleeve of her dress. But the smile soon faded when she remembered why she was in this state. What she'd done. "I… I didn't mean to hurt him," she blurted out, turning to face Gothel. Her hair wrap was so tight today she had a headache, but she was afraid to loosen it and hurt Gothel. Headaches, she could deal with. Murder? She wasn't sure how she'd live with it. "I… I t-tried to get away while he was sleeping, but he'd set up some sort of trap, and he grabbed me, we struggled—"

"Hush, child," Gothel soothed, tracing her fingers

over Annice's knuckles. "You needn't explain. It was an accident."

"But…" Annice spluttered, trying to form words. "But I *killed* him!" A new sob erupted from her lips.

Gothel thumbed at her cheeks to wipe her tears away. "Shh. Now do you see, my darling? I was trying to protect you from this. I never did this to make you unhappy."

"I know. I see that now." Thank the light she hadn't harmed Cyrus.

"Listen to me. I won't hire another guard. But you mustn't see that young man again. We don't want this to happen to him, do we? I know it'll break your heart. But less so than if…"

She didn't need to finish; Annice knew the rest. A broken heart from missing Cyrus being around was better than him being dead.

"I understand," Annice whispered. "But can I write him one more letter? To say goodbye properly," she added hastily. "I won't see him again. I don't want to hurt him like I did that man."

Gothel considered for a moment, then, looking into Annice's tear-stained face, she must have seen something genuine and truthful. "Very well. I'll bring your writing utensils back tomorrow."

"Thank you." Annice wanted to hug her, but held back, and instead squeezed her hand as tightly as she could.

Gothel smiled back.

Dear Cyrus,

I'm sorry I haven't written to you, or answered your recent letters. My mother found out I'd been writing you, and she wasn't very happy. With good reason. It's been such a joy being your friend and getting to know you, but I think we must end our correspondence and our meetings here. It's too risky for you to be around me. I hope you can understand, and I truly do wish you the best in life. Give my best to Bellamy, and Max, too.

Yours,
Annice

It was a rainy night, several days after she'd sent her farewell letter to Cyrus. Gothel had visited each day, putting off work and closing up the flower shop to be there for her daughter, staying well into the evening hours. Annice was appreciative. She didn't want to sit around moping, thinking about Cyrus. Still, he crept into her thoughts, regardless of whether she was occupied or not. She wondered if he'd received her letter, and if he felt hurt. Would he miss her as much as she missed him? She hadn't realised how much she'd enjoyed his company until it was wrenched away from her.

Tonight, Gothel had just gone home. Annice had the shutters open, giving her a view of the softly falling rain and the moon ringed in a hazy glow as it peeped from behind a grey cloud. The treetops were swaying slowly, shedding the occasional leaf in the wind. At first, she thought the tiny thing fluttering towards her was one of those leaves, until it drew closer and she realised it was a tiny bluebird with a letter clamped in its beak.

Excitement blossomed in her chest. Could it be Cyrus writing her back?

The bluebird letter carriers were strong, given the amount of magic contained inside their little bodies, so it fought the wind with no problem at all, and flew into her sitting room in a solid, straight line. Landing with a dull thud on the table, it fluffed its feathers and held itself aloft until she hurried across and pulled the letter free from its beak.

"Thank you," she told it, and the bird fluffed itself up further.

There was a bowl of grapes in the kitchen, so she fetched some for the bird to peck at while she retrieved her letter opener. The writing detailing the address of her tower didn't look familiar – it wasn't Cyrus, she realised, her heart sinking. Annice sliced into the creamy paper in one smooth motion, curious as to who it could be.

She gasped. It was one of the apothecaries she'd

written to overseas, after Cyrus had given her the addresses.

Dear Annice,

Thank you so much for writing us here, and all the way from the Kingdom of Lumen. I visited once many years ago, and the goddess of light really does shine there as they say. The glowing plants are one of my fondest memories!

But I digress. You asked if we had any knowledge of the rampion flower and its properties. I'm surprised you don't already know, if you've encountered the rampion. There's a simple cure to the rampion's curse, native to and found abundantly in your kingdom: the glowing kingcups I so admire! Their petals are edible, and counter the rampion's effects.

I'm not sure why local apothecaries in the kingdom didn't inform you of this, although perhaps they were still in training and made an error. It's not common knowledge amongst citizens, as the rampion is much rarer than the kingcups, but most botanists and apothecaries would be aware of it, if you asked their advice. It would be the first port of call for treatment. Regardless, I hope my letter helps you with your studies. If you have an interest in travel or study abroad, or even in magical arts, perhaps one day you might study here at our university.

Yours sincerely,
Professor Arcus Faust
Elrune University of Magical Arts
Kingdom of Elrune

The paper trembled in Annice's grasp, the words swimming before her. Dizzy, she backed up, leaning against the stone tower wall. A simple cure. Surely not. This had to be a mistake. She'd spent her entire life in this tower, or thereabouts; if there was a simple cure, she'd know about it.

Unless Gothel lied, said a nasty little voice in the back of her mind.

—◦◦◦—

Why would Gothel lie? Annice couldn't understand it. Maybe it was a mistake. The apothecary she spoke to might have been in training, as Professor Arcus Faust had said. Either that, or Gothel had misheard the answer. There was just one problem. Gothel claimed she'd visited every apothecary in the Kingdom of Lumen and none of them knew of a cure. The professor was from a well-respected university of magical arts; he had no reason to lie. He didn't know Annice and he didn't have anything to gain by lying.

What reason would Gothel have to lie? To keep her in this tower, she supposed. But to what end?

Gothel had kept her away from Cyrus. She'd kept her away from potential friends, from living a life.

Coldness washed over Annice. Had Gothel been so protective of her that she'd fabricated this endless, uncurable curse to keep her here?

Why hadn't Cyrus or Bellamy told her the rampion curse was curable? Then again, perhaps they hadn't known. They weren't from this kingdom originally, where the flower originated, and they weren't apothecaries or botanists either – the letter had said it wasn't common knowledge amongst citizens.

The cold feeling inside her changed to angry heat. She almost balled the letter in her fist, but stopped herself. This was her proof. There *was* a cure. It was precious. Something new was fizzing inside her alongside the anger – possibility. Hope. She tucked the letter back into the envelope, and placed both in her pocket.

The bluebird was watching her expectantly with tiny, beady eyes, having pecked apart two full grapes.

"Thank you," she said. "I don't want to reply at the moment."

The bird took off, back into the night and sheets of rain. She watched it go. It would be flying over the horizon, over the sea, to another kingdom where the professor was. If she could find this kingcup he'd mentioned – which was apparently abundant – she could take flight, too. She could leave this tower, go into the forest, go as far and wide as she wanted, with nothing and no one to hold her back.

She could be with Cyrus. The image of a travelling wooden caravan, pulled by Max, a tiny home built inside for them both, nearly floored her. Her heart ached for it, to travel with him and get to know him better. Maybe their friendship could blossom into something more after all; maybe she didn't have to hold herself back.

If she just found the kingcup.

She needed to leave the tower.

Gothel would be coming back tomorrow, she'd said. When should Annice go? She pressed her fingertips to her cheek, thinking. If she didn't go now, she might lose her nerve. Gothel might start to suspect something; Annice had never been very good at hiding her emotions from her mother.

It was still raining out, but now only drizzle. She made sure her hair was wrapped as tightly as possible without hurting, and hurried around the tower, gathering up some things in a satchel. She still had Cyrus's address at the inn, thanks to Gothel agreeing to let her say goodbye.

Once she was ready – wearing puffed trousers, a blouse and a cloak this time to make it easier to climb and to keep her warm and dry – she stood, surveying the tower interior with a mild lump in her throat. What would she do when she found the flower? This was her home. She felt like she was abandoning it somehow by leaving to find the kingcup.

She knew she needed to do this. This was her chance to put the curse to rest, to live the life she'd always wanted. As she looked around, she silently thanked the tower and everything in it. For keeping her safe, and warm, and occupied, all these years. Looking at her books made her heart wrench. Before leaving, she took one of her favourite novels – a small-sized one, easy to carry – and tucked it into her satchel. It was one she'd read over and over again when she was feeling sad and alone; it held a special place in her heart. She'd at least take a small portion of this home with her wherever she went. In case she couldn't return.

Adjusting the satchel across her body, she stepped out onto the balcony, and into the drizzling rain.

Chapter Seven

By the time she reached the forest edge, she was panting, both with nerves and from her climb down the side of the tower. She'd had to climb sideways slightly, to find ivy that her hair hadn't destroyed last time – most of the ivy near the bottom of her balcony had been reduced to ashes. Her arms and fingers had ached before she even started descending.

She'd lit the lantern she'd pulled from her satchel while sheltering under the balcony from the rain. At least this time there were no guards to stop her. She felt a guilty lurch inside her, wondering about the dead guard's family, but tamped the feelings down. *Later. You can think about that later.* She needed to move fast, and find Cyrus at the inn before tomorrow. She didn't even know how far away it was. Stuffed inside her bag was a map of the area – she'd had plenty of travel books to choose from – but she might not need it yet. There was a road on the other side of this forest, and there were bound to be signs pointing the way.

Her boots squelched over damp leaves as she headed into the trees. Her heart was pounding at the base of her throat, and there was a buzzing feeling in her head. She was outside, going further than she could ever remember going. For a moment she thought she might be sick with the anxiety of it, her head spinning. Annice paused by a tree, steadying herself with a hand on the bark, and took some deep breaths. It felt strange under her fingers, the etched lines, the aged bark. The forest was a mass of trees but it was peaceful, the leaves rustling, branches crunching underfoot. She breathed in the scent of damp, earthy air, so different to the stale summer air of her bedroom.

"I'm outside," she said quietly, as if telling the trees, and a wide smile stretched over her face. "I'm really here."

She couldn't believe it. She wasn't even afraid – she marvelled at the shadowy shapes of the trees, the sight of an owl perched on a branch, eyes glowing yellow. When a wild rabbit crossed her path – shining orange in the light of her lantern – she laughed, watching a bobbly, bushy tail disappear into the dark.

She kept walking. She'd been able to see the distant road snaking into the distance from her tower so it couldn't be far. One foot in front of the other, and she'd get there.

The forest was like a breathing being, its leaves whispering *shh* sounds around her in the wind and rain.

As she moved deeper in, her initial thrill gave way to anxiety. There could be anything lurking in the trees. It didn't even have to be an animal – if she disturbed another person who wasn't expecting her, some bandit or other… Annice reached into her satchel for the knife she'd brought from her kitchen, and held it aloft.

Something crunched in the bracken behind her and there was a scrabbling sound. Annice squealed and jerked forwards, almost stumbling over an outstretched tree branch. Something skittered out of the gloom, a brown furry creature, and vanished, the sounds of its claws fading.

Wildlife. She'd scared it more than it had scared her. She laughed again – so many emotions in a few minutes. Was this what being in the real world was like?

It seemed to take an aeon, but soon the trees began thinning, and through an opening she saw the clouds dappling the sky. The ground beneath her grew sparse, the bracken and shrubs backing away – and there was the road! She'd never been so happy to see a dirt track.

"Made it!" she muttered. She *was* capable. Gothel never gave her enough credit. She could do this.

Annice hesitated, looking left and right. Which way should she go? Stuffing her knife back in her satchel, she fumbled for her map, trying to hurry – it was getting damp in the soft rainfall. Holding it up to the orange lamplight, she searched the many intersecting lines.

She had to go right. The dirt track would lead her a good way north-east. Then she'd take a second road right which would take her directly into the heart of the kingdom, where the palace was, and all the major restaurants and shops – and Cyrus. Her insides tingled with excitement. What would everything look like, in the centre of the kingdom?

She also knew Gothel lived there, and she could only hope she was at home sleeping, and that she wouldn't bump into her.

In the darkness she couldn't fully appreciate the sights, like hills on the horizon, or the small details of the roadside she might be missing. But she was *away*. Away from her tower, somewhere different. The air was damp with rain and she breathed it in. Soon she'd be in the thick of things. The shops and restaurants would probably still be open – it wasn't late enough for them to be shut yet. What would people look like? What would it *feel* like, to be there, amongst other people, for the first time? Would there be music, dancing?

Her anticipation was quickly smoothed over by self-doubt. She had to focus. She needed to be mindful so she didn't hurt somebody. She didn't have a kingcup yet.

The dirt track finally led her to rows of boxy buildings with sloped roofs; it was like another world and she started grinning again. Lit lamps were encased in glass, dotting the cobbled streets. The pathways sloped up and away, left and right, a maze of activity. Further in, she heard music, and raucous laughter and cries of joy. Still distant, but there. It was like a scene from a storybook, like nothing she'd ever seen. An illustration, come true.

People. *Life*.

This must be a residential district. Her map had told her it wasn't a main entrance. It was quiet. Some of the windows were in shadow; in others, candles and lamps danced. She wanted to look inside – to see how other people lived.

A cat slunk into an alley close by and she rushed over to it – she'd never seen one up close – but it ran away, tail vanishing over a wall, and she beamed. A sign nearby pointed to the main square and marketplace.

"Thanks, cat," she breathed.

That would be where she'd find Cyrus.

The rain had stopped. She knew she was close because the streets had filled up. Cafés and restaurants lined the streets. Windows were lit with dazzling arrays of lights and small white-painted tables were positioned on the cobbles, where people ate and drank and laughed. Annice had never smiled so hard in her life, and her heart was jumping with excitement. She'd never seen so many interesting things and people in one place. Buxom women in frilly dresses and wide summer hats, holding matching umbrellas to stave off any returning rain. Men leaned across tables and drank from goblets, wearing sleek purple tunics with gold buttons and smart boots up to the knees. A few children were out, chasing each other up and down the street, wearing flat caps on their heads and giggling. The sight of them made something well up inside Annice and she caught herself fighting back tears of joy. The last time she'd seen a child, she'd been one herself.

She could stand here for hours, soak it all in. But she was still cursed; she had to fix it.

The inn Cyrus was playing at was at the top of a street sloping upwards, lined by tailor's shops and seamstresses and baker's shops, all of these closed up for the evening and darkened. A cluster of people walked down the street at the top, arms slung around each other's shoulders, singing in drunken slurs. One of them was shirtless and being hauled along by his friends. Annice smiled faintly at their antics but she kept her distance; she still wasn't used to being around people.

They must have come from the inn. She could hear music – what sounded like a fiddle playing. She hurried up the street, following the noise.

Turning the corner at the top, she saw the inn. It was nestled at the bottom of a hilly mountain rising up at the back of the town, leading to another row of houses, encircled by trees. The inn was a tall, three-storey place with an arched roof and curving windows, each one lit by candlelight. The double doors were thrown open, yellow light spilling out onto the cobbles. Roars and laughter echoed out into the street. Men and women were gathered in the doorway, goblets and tankards clasped in hands.

Annice sucked in a breath, chest tight with anxiety, and not just because this was risky, with her hair and her curse. But because she'd never been around so many people. The thought of walking over to them made her throat constrict.

But she knew she could do it. She tried to hold on to the thrill she'd felt in the forest.

She was lingering near the street corner and a closed-up butcher's shop. The inn's sign was swinging and creaking in the breeze, barely audible over the sounds of the punters crying out and slamming goblets on tables.

A great cheer went up inside the place, and feet stamped. Applause broke out. Were Bellamy and Cyrus performing? Maybe they'd just finished up. She grinned again, longing to go inside but knowing it was risky with her hair.

Soon the cheers died down and the ruckus quieted. Many of those gathered around the doorway began to drift away, either further inside the building, or away from the inn completely, having finished their drinks and entertainment for the night.

A figure stepped out into the yellow glow falling across the street – one she recognised. He was wearing a glittery green-and-gold tunic, and had a dusting of gold eyeshadow across his eyelids, which shimmered in the night.

Annice hurried forwards. There was no one else around for now.

"Bellamy?" she said, drawing closer and lowering her hood. Her wrap must look ridiculous to him, like a tall cocooned insect perched on her head. She'd used a thicker material to be safe.

"Annice?" he said. He'd only seen her once, so she was surprised he remembered her name. Cyrus must have talked about her often enough for the name to sink in. The thought made something inside her stir. "What are you doing here?"

Did he know about her curse? His eyes drifted to her wrap but he didn't mention it.

"Is Cyrus inside?" she asked. "I need to speak with him."

"He's gone upstairs to put away the instruments. I came out to smoke." He waved a pipe, which she hadn't noticed him holding in the shadows. "You can go inside if you want. We're the third room on the second floor."

"No, I…" She hesitated. He mustn't know. Cyrus hadn't told his friend a thing. She hadn't explicitly told him to keep it a secret, but she was touched that he'd chosen not to reveal her personal information to his friend without her permission. It spoke to the kind of person he was. Genuine, and not one to gossip about something that wasn't his to talk about.

"Do you want me to go fetch him?" Bellamy asked, glancing back over his shoulder at the doors. "I know it can get rowdy in there. It isn't everyone's favourite place." He followed the words up with a wide, toothy grin, and she was glad he'd assumed she was anxious about the crowd.

"Yes, please," she said breathlessly. "It's important."

"Alright. Give me a moment."

She nodded, and he disappeared into the clusters of people gathered around the doorway, and seated inside the inn.

Annice drew back against the buildings again as she waited. She didn't want to brush up against anyone who might walk past, despite how carefully her hair was wrapped.

Soon, Cyrus was there, pushing his way through the inn doors towards her. When he approached her, he walked into the light of a street lamp, and her breath caught. She'd almost forgotten how lovely he was – his olive-toned skin, the scattering of stubble across his face, long smooth hair. He was dressed smartly in dark clothes, and a single silver earring glinted in one of his ears.

His mouth was hanging open as he looked at her, exposing teeth. She couldn't help but stare at his lips.

"What are you doing here?" he managed. "You… you left the tower!"

"I know," she said, trying to control how husky her voice sounded. She cleared her throat. "I have to tell you something." She looked behind him as a group of three women left the inn, laughing, arms linked and their skirts swishing. "Is there somewhere… quieter we can go?"

"Come on," he said, jerking his thumb in the opposite direction. "I know a place."

She nodded, following his lead down the winding streets, keeping her distance. He kept looking back, as if to check she wasn't a mirage. She didn't blame him. She'd been so adamant about how much of a danger her hair was, how she'd never left the tower. And here she was, showing up at the inn. He must be so confused.

He led her to a small park built into the town – it had a metal gate, allowing them to step into narrow pathways lined by neatly planted trees and blooming flowers. Benches were scattered about, and she could hear a fountain trickling somewhere close by.

They weaved their way deep into the gardens, until the stone fountain came into view, a sprawling circular construction with a statue of the goddess of light standing atop it. She was holding a miniature sun, her hair falling down her back in a single braid. Water poured forth from stone jugs positioned around her feet.

Cyrus sat on a bench behind the fountain, and she joined him, keeping a large space between them.

"So," he said. "What's all this about? Why did you leave the tower? Why did your mother write to me saying not to contact you?" He trailed off. She knew what he meant. He was asking why she'd suddenly decided to cut him off.

She told him everything. What she'd been told all her life about the rampion curse, how Gothel had hid things from her, what she'd found out from the apothecary overseas. When she'd finished speaking, Cyrus looked grey. He made a move as if to touch her, to comfort her, but stopped himself.

"I had no idea," he said quietly. He cursed and balled his fist, slamming it onto his knee. "If I'd known…!"

"You weren't to know," she said softly. She leaned across for his hand, brushing her fingers against it lightly, then drawing back.

"I've been here long enough! I should have heard… or done my research."

Annice shook her head, smiling slightly. "No, you're not at fault. Only a botanist or apothecary would know. But my mother…" She heaved a shuddering breath, fighting back tears. "Why would she *do* this? Lie to me like that? For all these years."

"I don't know," he said, and straightened up, looking her straight in the eye. Her stomach somersaulted. "But I'll help you find the kingcups. We can go right now. If they glow, it'll be easier to find them in the dark anyway."

She nodded. A fresh realisation hit her. "I didn't even have any books at home, on botany, or flowers and herbs in the area… I'd asked for them before. But she'd always say the library didn't have them, or she'd read them before and they wouldn't help. She never let me write to the library myself, either. She wouldn't give me the address."

A frown made Cyrus's brow crease with three straight lines. He said nothing.

Annice's thoughts churned. The extent of the lies ran deep. She felt like her chest had been sliced open. She loved Gothel; she was her mother. And she'd betrayed her, imprisoned her like some kind of animal. The darkest curse placed on Annice had perhaps not been her hair, but the deceit that kept her trapped. Tears welled up, and she couldn't stop some from spilling out.

"Hey," Cyrus said. He shuffled closer, grasping her hand. She flinched, but he was keeping enough distance, so it felt safe. His hand felt warm and smooth. "Don't cry. We'll figure this out. First of all, though, we need to get rid of the curse. Shall we go? Max is tied up in the stables at the back of the inn. We can take the side path there. You'll have to ride behind me, though. Is that okay?"

Self-consciously, she reached a hand up to the hair wrap. She could never be certain it wouldn't unravel, especially on horseback. Her heart jumped at the thought of riding Max. She'd dreamed of riding a horse since she was a child. The emotions warred inside her: the fear of hurting either of them, and the excitement of riding.

"You can't go fast," she said. "It's too risky. We have to go slowly. If I jostle about… Promise me. I don't care how long it takes."

"Don't worry, I won't go fast."

"How are we going to find the kingcups?"

"The inn has books on the local area, for travellers. Mostly maps and guides, but I can ask if the innkeeper has any on botany. Failing that, inns are good places for sourcing information." He grinned. "Someone will know."

"Okay…"

"Come on. You can wait in the stables with Max while I go inside. They're always quiet at night."

"What will you tell Bellamy? I know you didn't tell him about my curse." She paused, swallowing, her throat dry. "Thank you. For trying to protect my privacy."

"I figured you wouldn't want the whole world to know about it." His smile turned softer, his eyes warming. "It's your business. I let him believe you were shy. I can tell him the truth, or say we're going for a late-night ride."

She nodded. "The latter would probably be best for now." She didn't know Bellamy well yet, and she didn't know what was going to happen next.

After he rose to his feet, she realised she wanted to keep on holding his hand – and if they found the kingcups, she'd be able to do that.

Ignoring the swirling inside of her, and the warmth

in her lower belly, she followed him out of the gardens and back to the inn.

—◦◦◦—

She stood, alone, in the stables with Max. Cyrus had already gone inside the inn to find out about the king-cups. Annice was keeping her distance from the horses, standing across to the other side of the stables, away from where they were tethered. Max's eyes kept open-ing and closing lazily; some of the other horses were snuffling at hay. Tack was hung by the doors. Back here, it was quiet, but she could hear the distant sounds of chatter from the inn.

When Cyrus finally came back, he was smiling in the dim light of the moon peeking through a crack in the stable, and her mouth went dry. She was struck by the fact that they hadn't known each other very long, but he was going out of his way to help her. The kindness was written all over his face like a love letter as he beamed at her.

"The innkeeper pointed me in the right direction," he told her. "It's not far, there's a clearing in the for-est by a waterfall, full of kingcups. Remember, when I told you about waterfalls before? I've passed it on the way to your tower. I never knew the flowers there were kingcups."

So close. It had been so close to her, all this time – her means of freedom. She gave a shaky laugh at the irony of it all and reached a hand up to her wrap instinctively.

"I'll saddle up Max," he said, making for the tack at the back.

She moved out of his way, watching as he grabbed a saddle and reins. She didn't know the first thing about preparing a horse for riding, so all she could do was watch, with nervous birds taking flight inside her. She knew they had to ride, but she was fearful; she didn't want to hurt him before they'd even arrived. That would be awful, to have him fall to her curse with the kingcup so close to her grasp.

An image of the tower guard, reduced to ashes, almost floored her, and she took a step back. Cyrus was already opening the wooden gate to Max's enclosure and saddling him up, the bulk of the leather resting on the horse's smooth white back. Cyrus glanced at her over his shoulder, likely having heard the stones crunch beneath her feet.

"Are you okay?" he asked.

"I'm fine," she said, wetting her lips with her tongue.

"I know it must be nerve-wracking, but we'll be okay." He nodded towards her, eyes lingering on her hair wrap. "It looks tight enough. I won't go too fast."

It must be written all over her face, how worried she was. Annice gave him a soft smile, silently cursing herself for never being able to prevent her emotions from showing on her face. It was a miracle she'd been able to keep him a secret from Gothel for so long.

Gothel. What was she doing now? The tang of her betrayal was bitter in Annice's mouth. Half of her wanted to track down Gothel's home and bang on her door, demanding answers, but the kingcup came first.

Soon Max was ready for them, and Cyrus had led him out into the centre of the stable, the saddle hanging from his back, headpiece in place, reins dangling. A wooden stepladder was positioned beside him.

"Hold the saddle," he said, showing her how to do it, a hand firmly gripped on the front, where a slight curve formed. She copied him. "Good. Now climb up to the top of the steps. That's it. Now I'll hoist you up, like this," he said, cupping his hands to make a foot-hold for her. "When I boost you up, swing one leg over and plant your backside in the saddle."

Her cheeks warmed. "Right…"

"Ready?" he said, when she hesitated a beat too long.

"S-Sorry," she stammered. "Ready."

Lifting her foot, she placed the toe of her boot into the crook of his fingers.

"One… two… three!"

He hauled himself up, pushing her with all his might, and she dragged herself upwards too, pulling on the saddle. As instructed, she swung a leg over, planting herself firmly down. Max was higher up than she'd expected, and for a split second she felt unsteady and too far away from the ground. She gripped the saddle tighter, fingernails digging into hard leather. At least her hair wrap was secure. She'd felt it bounce on the way up, but nothing had come loose.

"You'll have to shuffle back to let me on," he said. "As far back as you can. And lean away so I don't clip you."

She did as she was told, shuffling until she could feel the curving back of the saddle digging into her buttocks, leaning herself away. She tried not to lean too much; she didn't want the wrap dropping off. It was an awkward, uncomfortable position, but Cyrus was quick. In one smooth movement, he'd climbed the ladder, swung his leg up – miraculously avoiding her chest and face – and dropped himself down in front of her.

"There," he said. "Wasn't too bad, was it?"

"N-No," she said breathlessly. She didn't know what to do with her hands, hovering awkwardly over her thighs.

"You'll have to hold on to me tightly," he told her. She felt him shift forwards, his legs moving. "I've put my feet in the stirrups – the foot-holders. There won't be room for yours but if you position your legs against mine and squeeze tight you should be fine. Go on."

She did as he asked, her cheeks hot. She already felt sweaty and they hadn't even started riding yet.

"A bit further. Good. Now, hold my waist."

Tentatively, she wrapped her arms around his waist

and squeezed. She tried not to let her head get too close to him.

"Let's go, then."

She felt his heels draw together in two sharp motions, and Max walked forwards, his hooves clip-clopping against the stones and paving. The swaying sensation of being on the horse was oddly soothing, but dizzying. It wasn't as high as being in her tower, though.

"I can't believe I'm on a horse!" she cried out as they left the stables, and Cyrus laughed at her delight. Max whickered, as if sensing her joy too.

They travelled across the dirt track Annice had followed to reach the town, skirting the edges to avoid a wooden cart tugged by two horses being drawn along the track. The driver cried out in surprise at seeing them, and the horses screeched, but Cyrus steered his mount expertly and they passed by, leaving the cart far behind them.

Soon they were pushing into the trees, sticking to a winding forest path branching off the main dirt track. Cyrus slowed Max, needing to consult the map the innkeeper had given him to find the clearing where the kingcup plant slept.

"I can barely see," he muttered, holding the map up to a slant of moonlight. "I think it's this way."

She held on as he steered Max to the left, deeper into the trees and the shadowed bracken. There was a sound in the distance like a river rushing, drawing gradually nearer. Wingbeats sounded in the air, and something rustled amidst the trees. Max trampled through the forest until the trees thinned out, the forest floor widening into a clearing bathed in pale moonlight. Annice's breath caught.

A huge waterfall spilled down from a clifftop, pouring its rippling blue waters into a miniature lake below, creating mist that rose up around the churning bottom end of the waterfall. At the top of the cliff, the sky formed a midnight backdrop of dappled silvery stars, and the moon hung there like the white of an eye looking down on them.

Scattered around the edges of the lake, and across the grass of the clearing, were dozens upon dozens of gleaming white flowers, poking into the air, their stems straight and luminous green. They looked like closed fists; only a tiny hint of the petals was visible in a slight pale blue cup shape around the rim of the flower.

She couldn't believe they'd been here this whole time. The cure she'd needed, right under her nose. She could have walked here if she'd known; it wouldn't have taken long. She felt a sudden urge to cry, a sharp tickle in the back of her throat and a heaviness to her chest. The one person she'd cared about, loved, her entire life, had lied to her and kept her prisoner. She'd been barred from a true life for so long, and for nothing.

Cyrus clambered off Max first, his boots sinking into the grass, and reached a hand up to her. "Are you alright?"

"It's…" She took a shaky breath. "I can't believe I'm here."

She set her hand in his, and he helped her clamber down – she tried to keep her hair wrap out of the way, and put a hand to it once she was on the ground to make sure it was still secure.

Come morning, if this worked, she wouldn't have to do that anymore.

No tower, no hair wraps, no constant cleaning up of loose hairs, no needing Gothel to bring her food or books. No more isolation, and dreaming of the world and its potential from behind stone walls. She'd be able to experience it all for herself. Everything she'd ever wanted to do and see.

Cyrus was standing still, waiting for her to move to the flowers. He understood that this was her moment, and she felt her chest tighten as she realised what a good man he was.

Annice padded across the grass to where the clusters of flowers began. Their glow was almost as bright as the moon. She walked right into the centre until she was surrounded by them on all sides, and they swayed in a slight breeze as if they'd been expecting her. A couple of glowing petals rose into the air on the wind, dancing around the clearing.

Kneeling down, she took hold of a stem, pressing it

between her fingers, and reached for one of the delicate petals. It broke off easily between her other thumb and finger. Even when she lifted it to her face, it still glowed, dazzling her eyes. When they adjusted, she could see the thin veins of blue running over the petal.

She didn't want to speak in case her words broke the moment, stopped this from working. Cyrus was behind her; Max was snuffling softly at the grass.

"How does it work?" Cyrus asked quietly.

"The petals are edible," she said. "So…"

Annice raised the petal to her mouth, popped it onto her tongue and clamped down.

Sweet flavour burst through her mouth. It tasted like a cake spread with icing and jam, melted right onto her tongue. She swallowed.

She didn't know if it was safe to unwrap her hair, but she had to know. With shaking hands, she reached up, unwinding the fabric from around the tops of her ears and forehead, letting it drop into the patch of flowers. Dark hair spilled over her neck and shoulders, down over her chest and to the ground, all moonlight and shadow. For one horrible sinking moment she thought it hadn't worked – the hair shouldn't be black as night anymore.

Then she noticed fine spools of white rising through her hair, from bottom to top. A glowing light winding its way through the strands. And where it moved, the hair was lightened, the threads of black seeping away like ink into carpet. It moved faster and faster, and she choked back tears as the hair glowed and turned golden-blonde, the light quickly encompassing her whole head, warm like treacle.

Annice turned around to face Cyrus. He looked awe-struck, his mouth hanging open slightly in surprise. Even Max had stopped sniffing and snuffling around the grass and was looking at Annice, blinking at the glow of her hair.

Chapter Eight

"It worked," she breathed. She looked down, lifted her hair into her fingers to be sure, ran her nails through it. The light was vanishing now but her hair still felt warm, and the goldness of it shone like a new coin. "Is it all this colour?" she asked him, not daring to believe it was all finished – that the curse was gone.

"I think so," he said hoarsely. He waved a hand. "Give me a twirl and let's see."

She spun around, her face breaking into a smile. As she went, she lifted her hair, making it ripple and fall across her back so he could check. Her hair was no longer as dark as the flower that had ruined her life. She was free.

When she was facing him again, he was beaming back, his cheeks full of colour and his eyes dancing.

"It's all gold," he said, and took a tentative step towards her.

"Wait," she said. "I have to test it." Happiness was blooming in her chest, fast and excitable, but she had to check. She dropped the hair she was holding, let it spill down, and she moved away from the flowers, towards the grass, kneeling down. She let her hair touch the earth, shook her head for good measure.

Gothel had always told her life would blacken and die beneath her curse, killing anything it touched; she'd seen that for herself. But the grass remained vibrant, alive. A beetle was marching steadily through the grass in the glow of the moon, and it walked right over her hair and disappeared into the clumps of greenery, as alive as it ever had been.

"It worked!" she cried. She rose to her feet, staggering in her haste to move closer to Cyrus.

He stepped towards her, until they were face to face, closer than they'd allowed themselves to be before. There was so much she wanted to know about him – so much they hadn't been able to do together or talk about when confined only to letters. He'd helped her with this, with getting her life back, and it meant more to her than she could express. The feelings swirling inside of her were new and confusing and exciting all at once. She thought again of the life he wanted, on the road with a family of his own, and for the first time it seemed possible that she could be the one at his side.

Cyrus moved even closer, and raised his hand to

brush the soft skin of her cheek. "You look even lovelier now," he said breathlessly.

The waterfall rushed behind them. Annice had wondered before what it would be like to kiss him. Now she could. But she also realised she had no idea what to do – how to initiate it, how to do it. Twenty-one, and she'd never been kissed. The curse had cruelly robbed her of experiences she might have had, and she would have to catch up. A new feeling wormed its way into her chest, one that was uncomfortable. She may have pleased herself in the past, but that wouldn't help her here.

Cyrus seemed to know how she was feeling. His thumb moved from her cheek to her bottom lip, and she held her breath.

"I know you've missed out on a lot," he said huskily. "So forgive me if I'm being too forward, or rushing you, but I'd really like to kiss you. Can I?"

The word yes got stuck in her throat. She couldn't speak so she jerked a nod. His fingers cupped her chin, catching her at the end of the motion, and he leaned in.

His lips pressed softly against hers. Gently. She pressed hers back. She felt dizzy with the movement of lips upon lips, and almost bashed into his teeth as she tried to get it right. But soon it was like her mouth had always known what to do; the rhythm came and they found a cadence and she *liked* it. He wound his fingers into the gaps between hers. A heat spread low in her belly, and she felt like she was floating. For a long while, she couldn't stop, pressing closer to him, her body crackling with the rush of it, but then she pulled back, heart pounding.

They were both breathless. She hadn't known what she'd expected from kissing but this euphoria, this lightness, as though the ground wasn't there, wasn't it. A fluttering sensation far down in her abdomen. A *wanting*.

That would come later. Eventually, when she knew him better. She already wanted him to kiss her again. But Cyrus looked away, towards Max, deep in thought.

Her heart sank – had she been *that* bad at kissing?

"What's wrong?" she asked quickly. "Didn't you…?" *Didn't you like it?* She couldn't ask.

He glanced back at her, squeezing his hand, and beamed. "Sorry. I did – I could stand here and kiss you all night. But I was thinking… What are you going to do now?"

Annice bit her lip. Gothel. She would have to be dealt with. Annice couldn't run off into the sunset with Cyrus, because one question was gnawing at her insides, grating away at her very bones: *why?* She couldn't do anything, move on, until she had an answer. Why had Gothel lied to her, all this time? She'd always believed the woman loved her and the possibility that their relationship hadn't been what it seemed was like a crushing weight on her chest. How could she enjoy the rest of her life with this hanging over her?

She needed answers.

"I need to see my mother. She's told me where her cottage is before," Annice said. "She always talked about it. It's close to town, on the outskirts. Near Greenbrook Farm and the gardens."

"I know the farm, the gardens too. Bellamy and I played there at a wedding."

"It's called Thorn Cottage," Annice explained. "It's not far from the gardens. She likes to go walking there…"

"Then let's go find her."

"You'll come with me?"

"Of course I will. I'm not letting you see her alone. I don't want to upset you; I know you care for her. But we don't know what her motivations were – are. If we confront her about this, how will she react?"

"I don't know," Annice said honestly. Gothel had always been prone to outbursts, but usually sobered quickly and brushed them aside. In this situation, though, she wasn't sure. If there was malice behind what she'd done… Annice shuddered. She didn't know that. Gothel might have had a good reason. The only way to find out was to talk to her.

"Let's go," Annice said.

"Now?"

"I don't want to lose my nerve." If they didn't go now, Annice might never go. She was already so hurt by Gothel's betrayal; it would be easier to disappear, to put it behind her. The answers to her questions might hurt even more. She didn't know. But she would find out.

They rode in the direction of Greenbrook Farm and the botanical gardens, keeping to the lantern-lit winding dirt roads, the kingdom to their left. Rolling hills and fields sped by, the occasional cow mooing from the gloom. Annice had always wondered what it'd be like to explore the kingdom at night, and it felt surreal to be rushing over the weaving pathways lined by bracken and trees, listening to the sounds of the night, the pinprick stars rushing by overhead. It was like she was living in a dream, bound to wake at any moment, back in her tower, cut off from it all. A strange, pungent scent was in the air and she wrinkled her nose.

"What's that?" she called to Cyrus. Her arms were wrapped around his waist as she bounced atop the saddle behind him, her legs close to his. She could feel the warmth of him, as if she were sitting by a hearth in the winter.

He glanced back briefly and burst out laughing. "Cow dung! Something you haven't been missing out on!"

She took in what he'd said, then laughed herself, the sound echoing across the roads. He was so jovial, it made her feel lighter in the wake of what was coming: a conversation with Gothel.

Soon farmhouses were springing up in the nooks and crannies of the hills to their right, and on their left, the land levelled out into a sprawling mass of flowers, vines, archways and gates. The botanical gardens. In the night, she couldn't see any colour, only twisting shapes and leaves. They had to pause under a lamp to consult their map again before trotting off down some side roads to find Gothel's house.

As Gothel had told her, it was tucked away towards the back of the gardens, down a dirt track with a wide wooden gate marked with a plaque that shone gold in the moonlight.

"Are you ready?" Cyrus asked, dismounting and glancing up at her. His eyelashes were like spun gold.

"I think so."

He helped her clamber down and searched for a tree to secure Max to. When Max was tied up, happily munching on some grass, he returned to her side.

"After you," he said, opening the bolt on the gate for her. It squealed harshly and Annice wondered if Gothel would hear them approach, if she was even home. She half hoped she was out.

Annice led Cyrus up the track, and her breath caught. There were kingcups everywhere, illuminating every side of the path and lighting the way to the cottage, which sat nestled at the top of a short hill, embraced by a cluster of thick trees. The glowing white-blue flowers waved in the slight breeze, stems swaying.

Her face grew hot. She couldn't believe Gothel had the gall to have these plants here, at her home. The cure, right outside her front door. And she'd hidden it from Annice, locked away in a tower in another part of the kingdom like an afterthought.

The bubbling anger sped her footsteps, and she was soon closing in on the cottage. She paused a moment, hands clenched into fists as she took it in, nails biting into her palms. It was a squat, low building with ivy and flowers clambering for space across the brickwork, a chimney protruding from the thatched roof. In the light of the kingcups, she could make out that the door was painted green, with a silver knocker. There was a small front garden, overflowing with potted plants and herbs, and a low neatly painted gate.

Annice stomped over to it, shoving it open and striding to the door, hair flying behind her. She still couldn't get used to the golden hair flowing down her back. Cyrus was quick on her heels. Before he could say anything to her, she was banging on the knocker. Best to act now while the anger coursed through her veins. Anger was good; it was better than anxiety.

She kept banging.

"Yes, yes, I'm coming!" called a voice on the other side. Gothel, sounding irritated that she'd been disturbed.

There was the sound of a lock screeching, a chain link being moved, and then the door was open and Gothel was there, in her purple nightgown, the string tied around her waist.

When she saw Annice standing there, her mouth dropped open. Her eyes moved from Annice's face to the golden hair spilling downwards. Gothel made a strangled sound and shifted her attention to Cyrus briefly, before her gaze flickered back to her daughter.

"What…" she choked out.

"I need to speak with you," Annice ground out. "*Now.*"

Without waiting to be invited, she pushed her way into the cottage, past Gothel. Cyrus followed.

Moving down a narrow hallway littered with coats and boots, Annice found herself in a square living room, filled with comfortable armchairs, a stone fireplace, and books stacked haphazardly onto shelves. More potted plants lined the window ledge and the corners of the room. It smelt like lavender and a musky scent she couldn't identify. Colourful rugs were sprawled across the stone floor and a pair of slippers sat by the fireplace, which was unlit.

Annice was shaking now. It was the shock of being here, in Gothel's home, of the kingcups outside. Gothel was comfortable in here, in front of that fireplace, all the while knowing she was telling a pack of lies to Annice.

"How," she said, her voice shaking, when Gothel appeared in the arch-shaped doorway, "can you even *live* with yourself after what you've done?"

Cyrus lingered close to her shoulder. He said nothing, but she felt him touch her wrist lightly and she was grateful for the support, to have someone on her side.

Gothel's face darkened. She crossed her arms over her chest. There was no remorse, no regret, in those hardened eyes. "What have you done?" she demanded.

"Me? You're the one who lied to me!" Annice shouted. She flung an arm towards the window, almost upending a potted plant on the fireplace. "The kingcups are *right there*! You knew and you let me believe there was no hope!"

"I gave you hope," Gothel hissed. "I kept telling you I'd save up money, didn't I? Speak to apothecaries—"

"There's something wrong with you. You're evil. You could have cured me—"

"I did it to *protect* you!" Gothel shrieked. Her icy expression turned on Cyrus. "I might have known *he* might have had something to do with this. But he can never understand the kind of love I have for you, after your foolish mother—"

She cut herself off. Annice held her breath. "You're… You're my mother," she said.

"No." Gothel shook her head, sighed, pinched the tip of her nose between her fingers. "I raised you. But I'm not your birth mother."

The silence in the room was cloying. Annice felt suffocated. There was too little air. Too many lies.

"Your mother was my sister," Gothel went on. "But she was a fool. She got herself pregnant with you before she'd even started building up her business as an apothecary, and her no-good husband couldn't help very much with coin. He was useless, sickly." She spat the words as if they were poison in her mouth. "I told her she could do better. But she was devoted to him, regardless. He kept getting worse. I said to her, *what about when the baby comes*? And she said she'd care for you both if needed, that you were her family. Foolish woman."

Annice didn't think it was foolish. It sounded like her *real* mother had plenty of love and compassion, more than Gothel had ever had. She couldn't bring herself to say what she was thinking: the story of her true mother was swimming in her head, catching in her throat.

"Well, of course she started to struggle when you were born. She had a lot to manage, caring for you and looking after her husband when his illness and pain flared. She needed help, but they couldn't afford a nanny, or a nurse for him." Gothel stared out of the nearby window, where the trees rustled. "I was running my own shop. I'd helped train her. Offered her a job when you came, but she couldn't take it. Too many responsibilities looking after you. And what happened instead? The rampion flower."

"What…" Annice cleared her throat and tried again. "What do you mean?"

"She couldn't see a way out. She said there was a market for carefully cultivated rampion – she could sell it to leaders of armies. If they only ate *parts* of the flower, she could provide cursed soldiers who could win any fight – if their hand was cursed, they could reduce people to ash with a single touch. I grew worried. I tried to talk sense into her. Her husband tried, too, he assured me he'd put a stop to her nonsense. Growing rampion is illegal, after all. But he couldn't watch her all the time, least of all when he was in pain and could barely walk." Gothel's lip curled in disgust. "She started growing it secretly. Small amounts at first. Then more, altering the plant as she needed to. It killed her in the end, before she could sell it – she suffered a fall in the greenhouse and landed on top of the lot. And your fool father died not long after of his sickness. The stress, I'd imagine, aggravated his illness."

Annice's mouth was like sand. Gothel told the story with a bitterness, a distaste, as though her parents were fools. All she'd heard was a sad, tragic story about a woman who had wanted to care for her family and had struggled to do so. She'd made a mistake, turning to rampion.

"They loved each other," she said quietly. "They loved me."

"*I* loved my sister too, and I loved you!" Gothel shrilled. "They didn't do a good enough job, protecting what they loved. It was their downfall. I wasn't going to be like *them*. They weren't hard enough; my sister was always too soft. I tried to tell her."

"So, what? You decided to lock me up and tell me lies? How is that any better?"

Gothel shook her head. "I was clearing the rampion from their house. It was dangerous for you. But

I suppose you had your mother's fiercely independent streak because you somehow got to it without me noticing, and I caught you eating a small sprig – the stem, with hair on. It wasn't enough to kill you, but you consumed enough to activate the curse in your body and thanks to your mother's careful cultivation, the hair stem concentrated on your hair. You know the rest."

"I don't know anything!" Annice spat. "You knew about the kingcups, you could have given me one of those when I first ate the rampion!"

"Your hair wasn't harming *you*. It was harming other living things: people, creatures. I saw an opportunity to protect you and I took it. You weren't going to end up like your parents, lured by the promise of love and family. That was the start for your mother, and it turned to greed and wanting more than she could handle."

Annice clamped her teeth together so tightly her jaw hurt. "You never loved me," she said, every syllable shaking. "If you did, you wouldn't have done this to me."

"I did this *for* you!" Gothel cried. She stared daggers at Cyrus. "And I see you still went the same way as your wretched mother. This is where it begins, Annice. I knew it the moment I found those letters. Love is as addictive as rampion, and it will claw you down with it if you aren't careful."

Annice stared at her. Was this the Gothel she'd always known? It couldn't be. All that had been smoke and mirrors. Now she was seeing the real Gothel, the one who was cruel and mean in order to be what she perceived as kind. But it wasn't kind. It was wrong, and her way of protecting Annice disturbed. Gothel had taken away her life up until now. Annice never would have learned the truth if she hadn't taken the risk of talking with Cyrus, of writing to the apothecaries. Her instinct to take risks had been right all along; Gothel had tried to smother it. Caution and carefulness weren't the answer: look what had happened to her. Gothel's idea of caution was to keep Annice locked away, never to experience anything or to love anyone.

Grasping Cyrus's hand, Annice knew what she had to do next.

"I'm leaving," she told Gothel.

"*Leaving?*" Gothel spluttered. She gave a cruel laugh. "With him? And where will you go? How long before he gets bored with you, or until there's a problem, and you find yourself struggling and scraping at the barrel for some kind of life? Happiness in love is fleeting, Annice. Soon you'll both be miserable like your parents."

The words were cutting, because Annice knew so little about relationships, and she was only at the beginning of her journey with Cyrus. But she knew one thing. She'd been miserable in her tower, and now she had a chance at a life, and all the risks that came with it. She'd take those over being lied to and manipulated, trapped in a tower and only experiencing Nethervale through books and letters.

"I'm leaving," she said again. "I won't see you again, Mo... Aunt Gothel. Goodbye."

She made for the door to leave the cottage. But Gothel was blocking her path in the archway, tight-lipped – with a plant-cutting knife clutched in her hand. Cyrus grabbed Annice and pulled her back into the room.

"You're going to stab me?" Annice said, low and dangerous. "Really?" She was trying to sound more confident than she felt – would Gothel do it?

"No," Gothel said, voice shaking. "But I'll take care of him, and take you back to your tower where you belong."

She lunged. Annice screamed, trying to stop her, but Gothel shoved her to one side, and Annice fell over a plant pot, tumbling to the ground. "Cyrus!" she shrieked.

Annice scrambled to her feet in time to see Cyrus grappling with Gothel, holding her by the wrists. With an almighty shove, he pushed her away, and she smacked her head on a shelf cluttered with plants and crashed to the ground.

"Mother!" Annice cried on instinct – even though she knew she wasn't her mother anymore.

She was motionless on the ground.

"Is she...?" Annice started.

Cyrus, panting from the effort of fighting Gothel off, moved across to Gothel and felt for a pulse on her wrist. "She's alive," he said, and checked the back of her head. "No cuts. I think she knocked herself out though. She'll have a headache, or a concussion, when she wakes."

Annice swallowed. Even after everything, she couldn't bear the thought of Gothel being harmed, and she was glad she was okay.

"We should leave now," Annice said. "I don't want to be here when she wakes up. Not after what she just did. I've heard everything I need to know. We can put some medicinal herbs on her head in case she needs them for the pain."

Cyrus nodded and clambered to his feet, helping her up.

When they'd seen to Gothel with the medicinal herbs, they headed outside, down the path to the painted gate. Annice kept her hand gripped firmly in Cyrus's as they walked back to Max, past the glowing kingcups and away from Thorn Cottage.

—❧—

It was the thick of night still, and they were back at Annice's tower. Cyrus had suggested they get some sleep and return in the light of day to collect her things, but Annice had worried that Gothel would come to the tower in search of them. Better to come back while she was still unconscious.

She stood in the centre of her living room on the stone floor, taking it in. There wasn't much she wanted to, or could, take. All the furniture would need to be left behind, and there were too many books to bring along on horseback. She'd allow herself a couple of favourites, enough to fit in a satchel. Padding across to the shelves, she scoured them. How could she choose? All these stories meant so much to her.

"Are you okay?" asked Cyrus. He was standing in the doorway by the stairs, leaning against the wall, arms crossed.

"I…" She shivered – the tower was chilly without the fire burning. Only ashes remained in the grate. "I never imagined I'd leave all this behind so soon. This is all I've ever known…"

He crossed the room to her side, placing a gentle hand on her arm. "Take your time."

She glanced up at him. He always appeared so calm – no worry lines on his face, a smile playing at his lips, those beautiful shining eyes studying her. "We hardly know each other," she blurted. Where had that come from? She supposed all her doubts had emerged, now she was standing here, preparing to leave. "I know so little about the world out there." She swept a hand at the tower window, at the midnight-blue sky, where clouds were scudding across the haze of the moon.

"You did fine, finding me at the inn," he reminded her. "And facing up to your aunt."

"Gothel," she corrected. She couldn't stand to hear the word *aunt* for that woman either. She wasn't family.

Aunt wasn't fit for someone who had betrayed her so cruelly. Every time the word crossed her mind, it was like a thorn stabbing at her heart.

"Gothel," he agreed. "Forget about her. You managed to come and find me. We broke your curse. You can live the life you've wanted now, whatever that may be."

"I have nowhere to go," she said, the realisation striking her. "No money. And I don't know the first thing about how to travel, or…" She trailed off. Nethervale was large and she suddenly felt so small, standing here under this roof, the only safe haven she'd known, surrounded by her possessions.

Cyrus took her hand. Her own fingers were cold, but his palms were warm, and he clutched at her and rubbed her skin. "Come with me," he said softly, leaning closer to her – he stood a full head taller than she did. "You can travel with us. You're good on your lyre, and at singing. We could use another member of our troupe – remember? I told you we wanted one. You could make money that way."

"I could," she managed, with a smile. "Are you sure?"

"Annice, I've never been surer of anything in my life. I want to get to know you better. Show you Nethervale and everything in it."

He looked hesitant, nervous almost, waiting for her reply. It was the first time she'd seen the hint of a frown crease his brow.

She beamed at him. "I'd love to come with you."

He grabbed her and swung her into the air, and

she laughed as he spun her around, her hair tangling around the both of them in a long golden clutch.

When he set her down, she caught her breath, tugging her hair free of their legs. "I want you to do something for me first."

"What's that?"

"Cut all this hair off."

"C-Cut… all of it?" he spluttered, his eyes following the hair from the top of her head all the way down to the floor. "Are you sure?"

"I never wanted it like this. I couldn't cut it, with the rampion curse. It always grew back to this length." She glanced down, levelling a hand close to her chest. "Maybe to here? That's more manageable, I think."

"Okay, but I'm not a barber, I'll have you know. Don't be angry with me if it's… less than perfect." He flashed her a toothy smile.

"I don't care. Hold on."

She fetched a knife from the kitchen, and she sat on the loveseat as he sheared half of the golden locks from her head, where they pooled on the floor like sunlight.

—◦◦◦—

Max was laden with a few satchels containing Annice's things: two of her favourite books, some clothing, her writing set and journal, a hairbrush, a few gold coins she'd found buried somewhere in the tower beneath the bric-a-brac, her lyre and song lyrics. She left her hair wraps behind, buried in the drawer beside her bed.

She was astride Max behind Cyrus now, her legs dangling close to her possessions, arms wrapped firmly about his waist. Her head felt a thousand pounds lighter, and she shook out her new hair as a breeze rippled across the clearing.

"Ready?" Cyrus asked her, reaching down and giving her hand a firm squeeze.

Annice glanced over her shoulder at the tower, shrouded in shadow, the ivy and thorns creeping up the side, the closed door. Once her home, now in her past. *Goodbye*, she told it silently.

"Ready," she said.

She knew she'd never see the tower again. But she had plenty of other places to see. The rest of the kingdom, and Nethervale, was out there – waiting for her.

Epilogue

Ten months later

The caravan rolled along the road, clattering over the dirt. Annice pulled back the thick curtain, looked out of the little window and smiled. Bellamy was sitting at the front, guiding the horses – Max and Bella. They'd painted the caravan red, decorating the sides with beautiful painted versions of instruments; that was Bellamy's work. He was almost as colourful as the caravan in his rainbow tunic and green hat, clucking his tongue at the horses.

Annice turned back to the caravan's interior. Opposite her, Cyrus was reading a newspaper by the other window, which was thrown open, showing a view of the trees and distant mountains topped with snow. She'd seen so much of the Kingdom of Lumen already, but the sight of those snowy peaks here in the south still made her beam with delight.

A cheeping sound drew their attention. A bluebird messenger was approaching, looping towards them through the air. It landed with a small thud on the edge of the windowsill and fluffed its feathers, a cream envelope stamped with a red crest clutched in its beak.

"Isn't that the royal crest?" asked Annice. They'd entertained some of the Royal Guard a month ago in a tavern – the guards had been on their way to the palace to carry out their duties – and she remembered seeing it stitched on their chests.

"It is," said Cyrus. He grinned at her. "You don't think word got back to the royals – about our troupe?"

"Open it!" Annice urged him, and she hurried across the caravan so she was sitting next to him amongst the colourful cushions, leaning into his side.

Cyrus kissed the side of her head, then took the envelope from the bird and broke the seal. He pulled open the letter and held it between them, so they could both read it.

Dearest Annice, Cyrus and Bellamy,

I recently had the opportunity to meet with some members of the Royal Guard, and they had nothing but positive things to say about you and your music. My niece, Lady Catarina Darlington, is engaged to be married to Prince Leonardo Rhydian in the coming months. I'm currently staying at Whitecliff Estate in the northern part of the kingdom with her. I've been searching for the perfect troupe to attend and play at their wedding, which will be held at the estate. If you would be so inclined, I'd love to invite you to perform. Catarina in particular enjoys the lyre, so I think she'd be quite taken with your Annice, and it'd be a lovely surprise for her.

Please write back at your earliest convenience to let me know if you'd like to play at the estate. I have enclosed the wedding dates and all the details you need.

Yours faithfully,
Lady Ruth Darlington

"It *is* about playing for them!" Annice exclaimed, grasping Cyrus's arm.

"Careful – I won't have an ear for music left if you shriek so close to me like that," said Cyrus, laughing. He looked back down at the letter. "Seems strange, though."

"What does?"

"There were rumours a while ago that Prince Rhydian was spending a lot of time with a woman from overseas called Pearl. I expected that to be the niece for a moment, but it says Catarina here. I wonder what happened to Pearl?"

"Have you been indulging Bellamy's gossip again?" Annice said, her tone light. "Maybe their relationship wasn't serious, or Pearl had to go home," she suggested, with a shrug. She could understand a relationship not working if distance became a strain eventually. If she'd been trapped in her tower forever, she couldn't have formed such a close bond with Cyrus.

"Perhaps. Anyway, what do you think about going to this wedding?" he said.

"What do *I* think? I don't know! I've only been playing with you for less than a year..."

He kissed the corner of her mouth. "Oh, we've done *plenty* of playing, that's for sure..."

"Not that kind!" she said, snorting, but she scooted closer to him, and he wrapped his arm around her.

"Maybe we should do some more now while Bellamy is driving..." Cyrus said huskily, his breath warm against her ear.

She laughed and batted his arm, giving him a long kiss as he pulled her into his lap. Her body thrummed as he snaked a hand to the small of her back.

"I know we were meant to go overseas soon," said Cyrus, more seriously, "but this could be a good opportunity. Our final performance here in the Kingdom of Lumen – for royalty." His eyes glittered. "Shall we do it? If you don't want to, I'll understand. I know you're keen to see the rest of Nethervale."

"You might be fine with it, but Bellamy would kill me if I said no!" She smirked. A giddy nervousness was making its way up her throat, and her words risked coming out strangled. But she knew what she wanted to do. When she was trapped in her tower, she'd seen the Royal Guard in the distance; she never thought she'd get the opportunity to be amongst royalty. How could she miss out on that?

"The rest of Nethervale can wait a bit longer," she said, linking her hands behind his neck. "Let's go to a wedding."

Cyrus's face brightened. "Let's."

Thanks for Reading!

Thank you so much for reading *The Darkest Curse*! Reviews are so important for authors – please consider writing one to help other readers discover my work for the first time.

Sign up to my author newsletter for extra content, and to receive updates about upcoming releases, including new books in the Nethervale world (coming soon!):

https://www.racheljrowlands.com/newsletter

About the Author

Rachel Rowlands is an author and freelance editor from North West England, and holds a degree in English and Creative Writing. She's worked on hundreds of books for publishing houses (including some of the largest in the UK) and for independent authors. Rachel grew up playing video games like the *Final Fantasy* series, and devouring any book she could get her hands on – and never grew out of her love for the fantasy genre.

Website: www.racheljrowlands.com
Author newsletter:
https://www.racheljrowlands.com/newsletter

@racheljrowlands – Twitter
@racheljrowlands – Instagram
@rachelrowlandsbooks – Pinterest

Printed in Great Britain
by Amazon

10403086R00089